LINNEY STEPP

LINNEY STEPP

DIANE GILLIAM

SADDLE ROAD PRESS

Saddle Road Press
Ithaca, New York
saddleroadpress.com

Book design and cover by Don Mitchell

ISBN 9781736525883
Library of Congress Control Number: 2022947796

Books by Diane Gilliam

Kettle Bottom
One of Everything
Recipe for Blackberry Cake
Dreadful Wind & Rain

To My Renshi Sisters: George Ella, Melva Sue, and Ruth

And to My Brother Doug

Contents

Done Deal

MARCH 1910

PEOPLE GET IN ALL KINDS OF TROUBLE and sometimes you can't tell whose fault it is, but you know whose fault it's not. Like when Mama's second cousin Pearl Chandler and her husband Virgil brought their next-to-least boy Robbie to live in the little lean-to room off the back of our house.

When Robbie come to help Daddy work our farm, on account of me and Betts both being girls and no good in the fields, that's when I got a picture in my head for that old word, hurt. I keep such pictures kind of like pages in a place in my head where I can go back to them, they are my only way of getting to understand certain things.

We'd been expecting them the day before, but you don't know long it will take people to get anywhere in March—in our part of Kentucky there can be snow still, or roads knee deep in mud from spring thaw, you never can tell. It was midday when Betts hollered from the front porch that they were coming, and we all went out and was standing in the yard watching them come up from the road in the wagon. Virgil was in the driver's seat and Robbie and his mama was sitting together in the back.

They both set still for just a minute after the wagon stopped, then Pearl patted on his knee in that way that means it's time and Robbie slid himself backwards out the tail end of the wagon. His mama handed him down a bundle, then clumb down out herself and just stood there looking at him. Nobody said a word. Virgil got down off the wagon seat and come over to them and put his hand flat on Robbie's chest, where the heart is, but Robbie turned his head and looked down at the ground. Neither him nor his mama would look at Virgil. She just stood on tiptoe and whispered something in Robbie's ear, then turned around quick and clumb back up into the back of the wagon. That took Virgil by surprise, looked like. He looked back at Robbie and said something to him we couldn't hear. Then he called out to Daddy that they figured to be heading right on back.

Robbie watched them out of sight. Stood stock still, and he wasn't nothing right then but his eyes, watching them go.

Once I met a doe in the woods in that starving time right between the end of winter and the breaking through of spring. Not a bit of green nowhere, the whole world brown and dry as an old creek bed. The doe looked at me, the purest look you could ever imagine. There wasn't no asking in it, nothing like that. Liked to broke my heart. I went to get her a cabbage out of the cellar, even though there was only four left and I knew Mama would know somebody'd took one. But the doe was gone when I got back.

I'd dreamed about her the night before Robbie come, and when I seen him standing there looking like that I knew why. I seen Mama flinch when Robbie turned his eyes on her once the wagon was out of sight. I tried to see what she was thinking, but she turned her back and covered her eyes with her right hand, how she does when she's telling something sad or hard. Daddy had his farmer face on, looking at Robbie's shoulders and back. Betts was fiddling with her dress and looking over toward the creek, like she'd just got out of all her chores.

They none of them ought to be doing him like that, is what I was thinking. I would never do him like that. I walked towards him real slow, trying to be easy, and picked up his stuff, all pinned up in a quilt, with my good hand.

I didn't know yet what all was going on. I had seven days of watching Robbie and seeing what it looked like before they told me.

Daddy was the youngest of the three Stepp brothers, Carl Stepp, the smartest and best-looking of them all, to hear him tell it. And he was handsome, anybody with eyes in their head could tell you that. He had them dark blue Stepp eyes and a square-jawed face with a good quick smile, and though he wasn't all that tall, he had a solidness about him that made you think he was a bigger man than what he was. His father favored him so he got the best of everything, including the good bottomland our house was built on. Our house was clapboard and painted white and plenty big enough for us. It set up a good ways from the river, but you could see the Tug from our porch, and the puddle-shaped greening that leaked out around it. Stepp Mountain, our mountain, rose up quick behind the house. When you're washing dishes and looking out the kitchen window you got nothing to lay your eyes on but hillside. Betts hates that, she can't wash a dish without carrying on about how dumb Daddy was to put a window there.

The house faces east, so there's just the shortest bit of time in the early afternoon when the slant of sun gets through into the little space between the mountain and the window. That little pane of light it sets down on the floor, pale that morning because it was so early in the spring, that's what I kept my eyes on while Daddy said his piece.

"So, now, girls," Daddy begun. He'd sent Robbie out to the barn to sharpen the plow blade. They'd brought us to the table, Mama and Daddy beside each other on one side and me and Betts across from them on the other. Daddy was hunched over a little bit, elbows spread, his forearms flat on the table and his hands and fingertips making a little tent like praying. He don't pray, though. This is his thinking pose. This is how he sits when he's figuring out how much money he's willing to spend on seed, or how much of what to plant in each field. He tapped his fingertips together a couple times and started again.

"So, now, girls. You know how Robbie's come to stay with us, now this makes sense. Virgil and Pearl's got five boys and they can spare him and I need him. This ain't nothing new, people do it all the time."

Mama was looking straight ahead but like she wasn't seeing a thing.

"Now Virgil and Pearl, they ain't got no girls," Daddy went on. I looked over at Betts and she looked at me like the house was on fire and only one of us was getting out. "And they got Pearl's mommy living over there with them," Daddy said. "That's Hesty. I reckon she must be your mama's aunt some way or another, anyway, that don't matter. The thing is, she's getting to where she ain't quite right, she's took to running off from the house and talking strange and such as that."

My place at the table was closest to the kitchen window, that little pane of light on the floor was right by my foot. Right there, just under the edge of the table was as far as it ever got, then it'd start to disappear from the bottom up. I put the palms of my hands flat on the table to steady myself, well, my good hand laid flat, the left one stayed bent and curled in, how it is. Daddy built this table. He built it inside the house after the house was all done. Four great big planks across and longer than my bed, with long benches on either side. They expected a whole crop of boys, him and Mama did, when he built this table. It's too big to get out through the doorway, so it's our table even though they only got us.

"Now, Linney, you're a sensible girl." Daddy kept on talking and tapping his fingers. Betts had been sitting straight as a rod, like somebody fixing to jump up and run, but when Daddy said this, I could feel how all the air went out of her. "You can see how it is," he said, looking at me out from under his eyebrows. "You go on up there and keep an eye on their Aunt Hesty so Pearl can do what all she needs to do, and Robbie comes down here and helps me get the crop in and makes it so I can keep up with everything's got to get done down here."

I should have made myself bigger, like the table. I should have hollered and cried and carried on about every little thing till they thought I couldn't take it, like Betts.

I sat there and I seen how every one of us sitting at this table had got some kind of deal, whether they made it themself, or agreed to it, or not. Daddy was not to be bothered, Mama couldn't be blamed for nothing, and Betts had to be took care of. I was trying to put words to what my deal was, and Daddy kept on talking.

"It won't be forever," Daddy said. "You'll do so good, Linney, I never knowed a more patient girl than you, nor kinder. They're going to love you and you won't need to be trying to do any kinds of chores will hurt your hand, just follow after Aunt Hesty, that's what they call her, and keep her out of trouble. You never been no trouble to nobody, honey, you'll do so good."

"Mommy," I said. My voice went high as a little bitty girl's and I couldn't remember last time I called her that.

She looked at me, but she didn't answer. She was not hardly even there.

What Daddy said, that was my deal, alright. No trouble. Nobody.

Betts was looking at me sideways, that sneaky smile with the corners of her mouth turned down, that only I know what it really means. That smile, I would not never forgive nor forget.

Daddy was running his right hand along the grain of table plank right there in front of him, feeling how smooth it was, and not looking at anything else. I'd have bet just about anything, he was thinking he was finally getting a boy to sit there with him.

"So, I'm supposed to watch on their Aunt Hesty?" I looked at Daddy to ask, once I felt my own voice back in my throat. I couldn't think what else to say.

"Well, now, I expect she is your aunt too. Let's see, if Pearl's your mama's second cousin, that means she's your third, I think. So that means Robbie and the rest of her boys must be your fourth." He looked at Mama. "Or are the boys your fourth cousins, Rose, and that makes them our girls' fifth cousins? Does that make them once removed? Or twice?" He looked back at me. "I never did understand about the removing."

I could not hardly believe he didn't hear what he was saying.

"Is that it, Mama?" I asked her. "Am I removed?"

She looked like she'd been slapped across the face.

"Is that it?" I asked again. I was going to make her say it.

She choked on it, like a piece of truth caught in her throat, but she said "Yes."

"It don't have to be forever," Daddy said again. But the picture in my head, of her saying yes, that was forever. I had to make her say it. I had to have a picture in my head to go back to, otherwise how could I ever believe it really happened?

That night I could not close my eyes and sleep in the room with Betts. I didn't know where to put myself in that house I'd been put out from. That was what it was, no matter how much sense Daddy figured it made. I wisht I could go sleep on the floor beside Robbie's pallet in his little lean-to room. All week long I'd been watching him, trying to see how to be good to him, and feeling so glad I wasn't him.

He was a full year younger than me, only fifteen, but already he looked like a man around his back and shoulders, and he was taller than any of us. That come from knowing how to work, Daddy said. He worked alright, kept his head down and did what Daddy told him. He ate like a man, too. I could tell Mama was surprised when he took not one or two, but four biscuits out of the pan at the breakfast table and a mess of eggs big as Daddy's. When he'd emptied his plate, that was the only time I seen him not looking like he was braced for anything at all to happen. He'd sit up real straight like he was stretching his back, push his plate back just a little, then put his arms down to his sides and rest a minute. Like just for that minute he'd got what he needed.

He had a nice face, ordinary brown hair and blue eyes like us, but set a little close together like cousin Virgil's. I'd not yet seen him smile. "That's my brother," I'd think when I seen him like that. "I have a brother now, there he sits."

I didn't know what he thought about us, though. He said please and thank you to Mama, and yessir to Daddy, as I was sure he'd been told before he left home, but not much else. I'd ask how he was, and he'd say "fine" or "good enough" but he never would look right at me. I figured being in a strange place and all it was too much to ask for him to be feeling friendly so I begun to hang back a bit. But I kept watching for ways to let him know I was on his side.

I needed somebody, too. Betts wasn't never on nobody's side but her own. I wanted a brother.

Come to find out, he knew all through that week that Mama was trying to make up her mind which of us girls to send back to Virgil and Pearl. She couldn't choose, that's how come they'd just dropped Robbie off. They meant to take one of us back with them, but Mama was still deciding. I didn't know whether to feel better because it was so hard for her, or worse because she thought about it so long and decided on me.

That night after they told me, when it got dark and I couldn't go back to my room with Betts, I got a quilt out of the cedar chest to sit on and an old shawl to wrap up in and I sat out underneath the window of Robbie's little room. The early spring cold outside felt right, like edges, walls that might hold me together. It was dark in his room, but I could hear him moving around a bit. I begun to rock and cry. Mama used to tell me a poem where a lady "made sweet moan," but there wasn't nothing sweet about what was coming out of me. I was starting to think I'd have to go off up the hill so I could thrash and wail where nobody could hear, but Robbie opened up the window just then. He put his forearms, elbows out, on the windowsill and his chin down on his hands. He didn't say nothing. After a bit, he dropped one hand down onto my shoulder.

"Why?" I said when I got enough control of my mouth to make a word.

"It was your Daddy's idea," Robbie said. "Leastways, that's what my daddy told me. He said they'd come from buying seed last fall in Paintsville and was seeing how much each of them had bought and talking about their places."

I wrapped my arms around my stomach and doubled over so my forehead was almost touching the ground. Last fall, that long, they'd been planning and knowing.

"Some of the men was talking in the Post Office about a railroad coming down alongside the river, over on the West Virginia side," Robbie went on with no feeling in his voice, like it was a story he'd told himself a hundred times. "There was talk about mining camps and new towns, and stores and boarding houses needing to feed all the men coming in to clear and lay the track. Then there'd be the ones that'd come in and stay to work the mines."

I knew this to be one of Daddy's favorite things to think about, he calls it progress. It's the twentieth century, he'd say, and he aimed to be part of it. He liked making plans, he wanted in on it. He liked to figure out work and money. I could picture him walking beside Virgil, half turned in toward him, bringing his hands together and apart to show him how big the different fields are, how high the corn grows, how much he could do, how much he could make—if only he had some real help to count on. He'd hire on boys from around, but they couldn't be counted on when their own families needed them, which of course was always when Daddy needed them most. If he had a boy of his own, he could plant more, sell more, plant even more. I could almost hear his voice rising up as it begun to dawn on him how it could be done.

"Our place, it's pretty but it's hilly," Robbie said. "It's not big like this, nor rich like this, with the river right here and all that good dirt washing down off the mountain every spring. Most of the time we eat pretty good off it, but we don't get nothing much extra to sell, usually just enough to pay for next year's seed. Thing is, Mama's about wore out, just keeping all of us fed is enough to keep two people busy in the kitchen about all day. When Mamaw could help, that was one thing, but now she's got to be watched, I mean, she'll take off into the woods or down to the creek and sometimes it seems like she ain't got no notion as to what might be out there nor how to get back."

He was quiet then. Long enough that I sat up and turned around to make sure he was still there in the window frame. His face was open and white from the moon. For the first time since he come, he looked me full in my face.

"It had to be me," he said. "It wasn't going to be Walty, Mama still calls him her baby and he's spindly yet, not ready for hard work anyway. I'm a real good worker, but the others are bigger and faster than me at most things. It made sense it would be me."

He straightened his arms and pushed back from the windowsill to where he was sitting up straight. His voice got thick and he said, "I punched Daddy in the stomach hard as I could when he told me. It was just us, we were fixing to plow up the piece of ground for Mama's garden and was just standing there a minute looking at it, and he said it. I run off the hill and stayed away for a day and a half so they'd see what they'd done and what it'd feel like to not have me."

Then he leaned back down, his face like before in the window frame.

"It was a done deal," he said. "Linney, it's a done deal."

I heard Mama open the front door and holler for me to come in. I wasn't moving from where I was, there with Robbie. I just got my brother and the deal that brought him to me was about to take me away.

"No, Mama!" I shouted it up into the air from my quilt under Robbie's window. I was seeing how his face must have looked when he punched his daddy. "No!"

Then the front door slammed and I knew what Robbie meant when he said it was a done deal. I'd never shouted like that ever before, for sure not at Mama. Even if they changed their mind and tried to take it all back, something was done.

Whoever I'd been so far, in this house—that was done.

It'd be another week before Virgil and Pearl come back for me. They'd have to wait, Robbie said, till they could get one of the neighbor women to come and stay with Aunt Hesty. The boys couldn't do everything around the farm and keep an eye on her at the same time.

I begun to try and memorize certain things. It was not the river's fault, nor the mountain's, and whatever pictures I could fix in my head would be the only way for me not to lose everything. When I took jars of water down to Robbie and Daddy in the cornfield in the mornings, I kept going straight on down to the river. The Tug was green. In its full times it was like a long green snake pulling itself along, going and staying at the same time.

I could go and stay too if I could fix in my head a picture of the exact curve the weep willow branch made with its tip and its new yellow leaves holding their own against the current. I closed my eyes to hear the splashy rush of it exactly. I picked up three round brown river rocks and put them in my pocket. Some says the river got its name from an Indian word that means 'forks of a river,' which I never thought much about, but I begun to wonder, where is the other fork it got tugged away from? It felt a little broken to me then and I loved it more.

I didn't run off and hide like Robbie did, but I quit doing chores for Mama. Instead, I went up the hill, walked the path up past the coal bank back of the house and up past the blackberry briars to a little clearing out of sight I'd found when I was twelve or so. I just sat. Knowing what was happening took up all the space there was inside me, it was hard work all by itself. I didn't know what I'd need when I got to the other house, but my clearing had two dogwood trees at its edges, and some greenbrier, and a rock in the middle that fit me for sitting on. At the end of my first day sitting up there, I drug my right foot in the dusty dirt around the edges of the clearing, making a circle like a moat in a fairy story about a girl whose father made a deal with the Devil, but she cried such pure tears when he came for her, Devil couldn't get near. I felt safer there after I'd done it. I only went back to the house when I was hungry.

"You are in so much trouble," Betts was sitting in the rocker in the front room and staring at the front door when I come in after that first day I made off by myself. Her whole face was pinched up like she had something that tasted real bad in her mouth. "I had to wash dishes all by myself and you know I don't do it good as you, and Mama was spitting mad when she seen what a mess I made of it."

Her and Daddy both, they don't even hear what they're saying. I walked right by her into the kitchen and got four biscuits off the plate on the stove.

"Get used to it," I said to her on my way back out.

As for Mama, seemed like she was the one afraid of me.

When I was down by the river or up in my circle in the clearing, I kept coming back around to what Daddy said about me being so patient and kind and no trouble to nobody. It sounded good, but far as I can tell, the only way to not be trouble for nobody else is to hold onto all the trouble for yourself.

It wasn't that I was thinking they ought to send Betts instead. They didn't have no right to be trading anybody away. I had pictures in my head for that wrongness. It had been going on for a long time.

Some years when Daddy'd go into Paintsville to sell the crop or to get the corn milled, we'd all go with him. If the money was good, me and Betts would get some pennies, usually two or three. But one year, when Betts was eleven and I was thirteen, it was five pennies—each. We stood beside each other with one hand out and Daddy went back and forth, putting one penny at a time in each hand, then he threw up his hands and told Mama we done cleaned him out.

"Oh, no, we didn't." We giggled and tickled Daddy all over, pretending like we was looking for the rest of the money he was keeping back.

"Now listen, girls," he said, wagging his finger at us. "Pinch every penny before you spend it and make them last all day." And he made like he was going to pinch us before he let us go.

We run off to the store fast as we could run, but when we got inside something slowed me way down. It was cool and darkish in there, and crowded with boxes and barrels and shelves piled full of goods. I could choose, that was the thing about those pennies. They were going to let me walk out of that store with something, and I was going to choose it. I set into looking at the little bins of spoons and knives and forks even though I wasn't thinking to buy that kind of thing. I wanted to look at every thing, knowing I had those pennies in my pocket. Betts went right up to the counter and pointed at a little box of fancy candies. They looked like little daisies made of sugar colored yellow and pink and blue, each one with a tiny little green leaf and a brown chocolate dot in the middle. There was six in a box.

"How much do those cost?" Betts asked Mr. Campbell behind the counter before he was all the way done counting out eggs for a lady with a basket and three little boys.

"Well, now," he said, joking with her a little, probably because he didn't think she was really going to buy anything. "How much you got?"

The men over by the stove were watching and laughing amongst theirselves. Betts was already pretty in a way that made men look. I left off looking and went up there and tugged on her dress.

"Remember what Daddy said," I said quiet-like, right into her ear.

She knew what was going on. She was preening a little bit and smiling that smile that pretends to be friendly but is really her way of laughing at you.

"I have five whole pennies," she said to Mr. Campbell, in her best I-don't-know-nothing-I'm-just-a-little-girl voice. It kind of stopped him in his tracks. I seen by his face he suspicioned he was getting took. Which he was. One of the men over by the stove sunk him.

"Didn't you say not five minutes ago that if any pretty little girls come in you'd sell them them boxes of candy for half-price?" The old man with the grayish beard grinned over at Mr. Campbell and elbowed the man next to him while they all laughed.

Betts handed over her pennies and got her box of candies and walked on out of the store while everybody watched. Mr. Campbell had his eye on me, figuring I'd want in on the trick.

"You too?" he said.

"No, thank you, sir," I said with as much dignity as I could muster with the men looking at me now and still having their laugh. "I'll be back." I'd have to walk around and clean that little scene out of my head before I could go back in and do like I meant to do with my own money.

Each of those flower candies was only about half a bite and Betts was looking at the last one before putting it in her mouth when I got outside the store. "Let's go find Mama and Daddy," I said to her and started off across the street without looking back to see if she was following me. We found them in the Post Office, visiting, the men standing up by the counter and the ladies sitting around on chairs and talking. Mama had brought a basket for dinner and it had been a long while since breakfast so we all went back to the wagon to spread out on the ground there under the trees and eat. Betts said she wasn't hungry, but Mama made her eat a ham biscuit anyway because suppertime would be a long ways off. There was the usual fussing and whining. "But it'll make me sick, Mama." She probably would be sick, but not on account of no ham biscuit. I ate fast and asked Daddy if I could go back to the store by myself. "I didn't spend any pennies yet," I told him. "I'm making them last all day."

Most of the men was gone to their own dinners when I got back to the store, so I could walk around real slow and look at things. Mr. Campbell called me "Miss" and told me to take my time and let him know when I was ready. I bought two ribbons, one sky blue and one soft green, and that was one penny. I walked around some more. I got a little stack of paper and a pencil, that was two more pennies. I might want to draw some of those pictures I was already collecting up in my head, or maybe write them down. I wanted to get some candy too, but I knew once I ate it I'd not have nothing to show for those pennies. I decided I'd spend only one penny on candy, and save the last one so I could hang onto that feeling that I could choose something for myself. I felt good, I felt rich.

Mama and Daddy and Betts were still back at the wagon when I got there. Betts was sulking and Mama was cranky that it had took me so long at the store, because Betts was sick. "I threw up," she said, like as if she was telling on me for something. They'd already loaded everything back into the wagon and we headed out of town. I had to sit on the sun side of the seat with Daddy so Mama could sit in the back with Betts and hold her head in her lap. Daddy was feeling good on account of the good money.

"What did you get for your pennies?" he asked me when we'd got out of town and settled into the slow part of the ride home. I told him about the ribbons, two for a penny, the paper and pencils, and the penny's worth of peppermints Mr. Campbell had weighed out for me then put a few more in. I heard Betts getting whiny in the back.

"That's only four pennies," Daddy said, and I told him about how I liked the choosing so much that I saved one of the pennies. "Good thinking," Daddy said, and patted my back.

Now Betts was sitting up and Mama was leaning up between me and Daddy.

"Hand me back them peppermints, Linney," Mama said. "You got plenty to share with your sister and peppermint is good on a sick stomach." I didn't want to, but I was not going to whine like Betts. I didn't want to do anything she would do. I passed them back. Mama poured them out in her hand, counted out half and gave them to Betts, then put the rest back in the sack and give it back to me. "Good girl," she said.

Before we got home, Betts had the green ribbon too. At least Mama let me choose my color first. Betts didn't care about the paper, so she only made a halfhearted stab at getting half of that and thank goodness you couldn't cut a penny in two.

That's one of my pictures for this wrong I'm trying to figure out—Betts in the back of the wagon with half my peppermints in one hand, my green ribbon in the other, and me knowing I'd been so careful and listened to Daddy and done everything right.

"Good thinking," Daddy said. "Good girl," Mama said. Good for what? For who? That's what I wanted to know.

The Chandlers lived up around Paintsville, on Hargus Creek, so I had a pretty good idea of how far I'd be going. I'd seen it on a map in the Post Office in Paintsville. It don't look that far as the crow flies, but a wagon don't fly and it'll take you at least all of a day to get there. If there's weather, or a tree down in the road somewhere along the way, or if you've got somebody that needs to stop and rest ever little bit, might as well plan on setting up camp for the night somewhere along the way because it will take more than you can do in a day. We'd never been to their farm, only seen them in Paintsville when we'd go up once or twice a year. It was in Johnson County and our place was in Pike County. It wasn't in visiting range.

I sat out under Robbie's window most nights while I was waiting to be took. After that first night, he clumb out the window and we sat together on the quilt, leaning our backs against the house and talking. He begun to tell me some things and I begun to tell him some things each of us thought the other one ought to know.

"First off," I told him, "Betts ain't nobody's friend. If she's acting friendly it's because she wants you to do something for her."

"I only been here a week" Robbie said, "but I don't need told that." Betts had already told him Mama wanted him to carry water in the morning, which was her job now that I was out of the picture.

Robbie was holding up his right hand, palm up, and rubbing at a new blister with his left thumb. He got it clearing and chopping wood for new rows Daddy was planning in the cornfield.

"I've chopped so much wood in my life," he said. "You all have got that coal bank out back, but we've not got coal where we are, we've got to have wood for everything. I can't remember last time I got a blister chopping wood, I didn't figure I had any soft spots left on my hands. They're used to my daddy's ax, though— that's the rub," he said, looking down at his blister. He put his hands down flat on his lap and let his shoulders drop just a little. He looked tired. "It's not that you're doing anything so very different, it's that you've got to do it with somebody else's tools, somebody else's way. That's what'll rub you raw."

I felt my shoulders draw up, I brought my knees up to my chest and wrapped my arms around them. If Robbie'd not been there I believe I would have keeled on over and rolled up into a little ball.

"The boys are alright," he said, "we ain't got nobody like Betts over home. Tom's the oldest, him and Daddy is joined at the hip so he probably won't even notice you're there. Danny's the biggest, though, and the friendliest. He'll laugh at you, but he don't mean nothing bad by it. Then comes Doug, he don't say much, he's more like me. Walty's the baby. He's in a hurry for Daddy to treat him like the rest of us, but still he'll let Mama get him out of some kinds of work if he don't feel like doing something real hard. Call him Walt and he'll be your friend from the get-go. Here's the good thing, Linney. With so many boys, and just Mama and Mamaw in the house, we all of us been taught real good to be respectful of ladies and to help with whatever they need. You'll have to ask, though, if you need something. I ain't saying we can think of what ladies need, but we're willing if you tell us."

I felt my arms loosen up a little bit from around my knees. I never been around boys, not really. I was kind of worried about that.

"Mama's good to talk and to laugh and be funny, leastways she was till she got so tired," Robbie went on. "And sad, I think. I think how Mamaw is now makes her sad. But I bet she'll get to feeling more like herself when you get there, and she don't have to worry with it all by herself. I expect it'll be nice for her to have another lady in the house."

Lady.

"Now, as far as Mamaw goes, I'm not going to lie to you, she's getting hard to take care of. There's some says when folks get old, it's like taking care of a little child. But she is not that, she is not a little child. She knows things, Linney. She knows a lot of things anybody would like to know, about plants and signs and why people's lives takes such and such a turn, and what happens right before you die and what comes after. It's just there's some things you'd think everybody would know, like how to open a door or don't pick up no snake, and sometimes she forgets that kind of thing. And she'll say things right out loud nobody else would say, like she wishes you'd stop talking, or private things I can't even tell you, you'll see. She ain't mean, though, it ain't like that."

We sat quiet for awhile. I tried to loosen up my mind enough to let some of what Robbie was telling me come in. My mind didn't want to loosen up though, on the inside I was still trying to fight it off. I tried to think what I could say to help him, but I couldn't find nothing good to say about Mama nor Daddy nor Betts, nor any part of it.

"There's a clearing up the hill," I told him. "If we can get up before everybody else in the morning I'll take you up there and show you."

We sat quiet another good while.

"Robbie," I said. "My heart is so hard against them, I think I hate them all. I'd give you anything I had right now, but I got no words except would add to the trouble."

"Well, now," Robbie said, and he took and held my hand, my bad hand, for I was sitting to his right, and I could feel the place that was rubbed raw on his palm. "You don't have to say nothing, I know you can't. You got to leave first, and be in the other place and still breathing before you know you're not going to die of it."

I dreamed about the doe again, the night Robbie said that to me about not dying of this. She was standing outside the back corner of a house, like a house in town.

She was not alone this time, she had a little spotted fawn with her, laying on the ground beside her with its head up and looking at me just the way the doe did. The fawn was under a little dogwood tree somebody'd planted by the house, so it had a little shade, just enough to cover it if it didn't move. It being a dream and all, the dogwood wasn't hardly bigger than a good size rose bush. Outside that bit of shade, everything was blazing hot sun and town. I think I was seeing it out the window of a house next door. When I kept looking, I seen the fawn had a chain around its neck, it was chained to a stake drove into the ground right by the trunk of the little dogwood. I looked on back behind the house to see if I could see whoever done such a thing. I seen the edge of the woods not thirty feet from the doe and the fawn. It was cool and green back there. There was a creek, I could hear it, and all the woodsy things, moss and leaves and scurrying things, everything that fawn needed was right back there, just beyond the reach of that chain.

Next morning at the breakfast table, with everybody sitting there, Betts said "Were you crying last night?"

"I hate you," I said. I said it flat out. It was that simple.

"Now, Linney," Daddy said, and that was all, he kept on eating.

Mama didn't say anything. What could she say, now that she didn't know what I might say back? She tucked her lips between her front teeth and bit down on them—a face she makes to signal us to be quiet—and shook her head. She got up from the table and walked out the front door. If I'd started crying then, I'd have never been able to stop.

"Now see what you did?" Betts said and took another biscuit.

I stood up and looked at Robbie for just a second and he looked back. I left my plate on the table for Betts to clean up and followed Mama out the door. I turned the other way, away from her, to go back up the hill to my clearing but I seen she was filling up the washtub at the pump. I stood there watching her arm go up and down on that handle fast as I ever seen it go. It wasn't even washday—then I got it. She was fixing to wash my clothes, so I could go, so she could get me over with. She was doing it to hurt me. I felt like I might fall over backwards. Then I heard a awful, choking noise coming out of the pump, only it wasn't coming out of the pump, it was coming out of me.

I run on up to my clearing. I needed to cry, and I did, I don't know how long. When it was over, I was laying in the dirt under one of the dogwoods and nothing was any better but there was a kind of calm come on me. Mama being mean broke something in me that'd kept me from believing I was really leaving. I sat up after a while and crawled on over to my rock in the middle of the circle. I sat on the ground and leaned my back up against the rock, my legs straight out in front of me and my hands in my lap. I was tired.

I was tired and I was worried about my hand too. I didn't think too much about it when I was here at home, but when we went into Paintsville or even to church, I would remember about it and feel funny. Mama always made me pockets on my dresses so I'd have some place to put it. They had to be big pockets because, what it is, my left wrist stays crooked down and my fingers turn in toward my palm. I can do most things one way or another, like prop a plate up against my body with my bad hand while I wash it with my right one. Not things like knitting though, or any kind of fancy work, or any really two-handed things like peeling potatoes or stringing beans. Most people get used to seeing it, but it feels bad till they do. Now I had a whole bunch of new people I was going to be living with, every day, and I wouldn't be able to keep my hand in my pocket.

I didn't even know anything was wrong with my hand till Betts was two or three. When it was Mama and Daddy and me, I seen their hands all looked alike but me being the only little one, I just figured mine was not grown out all the way. I must have been about five when I took notice that Betts's hands were both the same.

Mama was hanging bedclothes on the line and I was handing her up clothespins one at a time. "How long," I asked her, "till my hand grows out the rest of the way?"

However crooked my hand was, that's how crooked her face went and she stood there with a clothespin in her mouth, not answering. I got a bad feeling. I didn't know why it was a hard question. I let go of the bag of clothespins and tugged on her dress. "How long?" I asked again.

She squatted down to where her face was right to mine. "Linney, sometimes they don't grow out all the way. Sometimes hands just come like that." I felt my face pucker up and for the first time ever I tucked my hand behind my back. "How come?" I asked. "What's wrong with me?"

I don't remember what she said, nor do I have any pictures in my head for anything more about that talk. If I could remember what she told me, maybe I'd have known why she was sending me away.

I'm pretty sure that's when I started calling my left hand my bad hand. I'm pretty sure that's when I started trying to be so good. Anytime I seen Mama working, I'd start helping without being asked—even churning which is hard for me because I can't switch off hands. Anytime I seen Daddy tired, I'd bring him his coffee or the stool to put his feet up on. When your bad part is right out there where everybody can see it, you've got to put something overtop so it don't show so much. An apron pocket ain't enough. Being good wasn't enough either, or else I wouldn't have been up there in my clearing, coming to in the dirt under the dogwood tree.

I kept that calm from up in the clearing over the next couple days. I only felt like running once, when I seen my clothes up on the line, all of them, for summer and winter both. Mama was real quiet after that, too. She never did anything else meanlike, just walked around looking emptied out. You could still see the pretty girl Mama had been, behind how she looked now that she'd worked herself ragged. Her hair was brown and thick, and so straight that she couldn't hardly keep it knotted in the back, it would slip right out of whatever kind of twist she tried to fix it in with hairpins. When it straggled, it wasn't pretty and curly, it just made her look like she was coming apart. I had the same hair and she was always fussing at me to keep it back off my face. Her eyes were grayish blue and small, her nose was little and pointy and so was her chin—you could also begin to see what she'd look like when she got old. But she still had a pretty mouth when she smiled. I looked like her in my features, except I had Daddy's square jaw, which undid a lot of the prettiness. We had the same kind of body except for my hand, me and Mama, both of us about half a head shorter than Daddy, small but not delicate, sturdy.

Betts, on the other hand, looked just like Mama in her face and was slighter than either of us, in a way that seemed to make people think they ought to give her whatever she wanted. I figured Mama was in for a whole lot more work once I was gone, I couldn't see Betts doing how I did. Mama'd have more work wrestling Betts into doing chores than she'd have doing them herself. But I had better things than that to worry about.

Virgil and Pearl sent word by Henry Stokes, one farm down from us, that they'd be coming to get me toward the end of the week. They couldn't say which day, it would depend on when their neighbor Kate would be done enough with her work she was doing to come be with Aunt Hesty and the boys. My clothes was all done up and piled on Mama's cedar chest in the front room. I didn't have much else to think about taking except for my box Daddy made me to keep my papers in. He'd come across a pretty piece of poplar and planed it into a thin board he cut into pieces, then dovetailed and fitted into a box with a lid that opened with leather hinges. He carved my name in pretty letters on the top—Caroline, my given name, though they called me Linney—and rubbed it good with oil and give it to me when I turned sixteen. Daddy had Henry bring me some more paper and two new pencils back from Paintsville to take with me to Chandler's. "For letters, maybe," he said, then he smiled but not really and looked off over toward the fields.

That night I give half of the paper and one of the new pencils to Robbie, so he could write to me. He'd said he would, even if he wasn't very good at it. "Good don't matter," I told him. "Good ain't for what."

Next morning, I went to put the rest of the new paper and the other pencil into my box. I was standing in the bedroom, with the box open on my bed. I kept my ribbons in there too, those three round river rocks I'd picked up, and that penny I'd saved to feel like I could choose. I picked up the penny and looked at the top side with the face on it, then turned it over and looked at the other side, with the circle of wheat. I held it up to my nose and smelled the metal smell of it, then I put my tongue on it. It tasted a little bit like blood.

That's what choosing tastes like, I thought, blood. I rubbed it between my thumb and my forefinger, but I didn't pinch it. Then I thought, Mama didn't choose to keep me, but I could still choose something—and not just one penny's worth either.

I felt my body straighten up, the way Robbie's did that first night when he told me about punching his Daddy in the stomach. I would choose who I would be. Away from Mama and Daddy and Betts and how they got it all set up, I would be able for it. The Chandlers didn't know me. I could start over. I could decide.

I didn't know who I would be, my head felt as blank and light as the new paper in the box. I put my penny back in and carried the box out to where Mama was still fussing around my clothes. I set it down on top of one of the piles. "I'm done," I said. She kept asking me at every turn what else I might need and I told her "I don't know" so many times that after while I just quit answering and she quit asking.

Robbie got real quiet too, even when it was just me and him sitting out back behind the house after supper till the sun went down and it got too cold. It was going on three weeks he'd been with us, and him and Daddy seemed to be getting on alright. It felt good, Robbie said, to work a farm that was growing and to think about what all Daddy said about making money and making progress. Daddy'd even promised him a piece of money at the end of the season, depending on how the crop did.

"I miss Mama and Daddy," he said, and leaned his head back against the house. It was just getting dark, to where I couldn't see his face very good. "But seeing them now's going to hurt more than it helps." He leaned a little sideways, picked up a rock laying near the edge of the quilt and slung it straight and fast across the way into the coal bank. It made a good solid sound. *Thwack.* I started handing him rocks.

"I don't want you to go, neither." *Thwack.*

"I'm your brother now, Linney," he said. *Thwack.* "You're like my sister. Right?" *Thwack.*

"I am," I said. "Nothing removed about it."

We didn't know Mama was back there in the kitchen with the window open till she hollered at us to stop throwing rocks and come inside to bed. We waited till the house was quiet and dark so Mama wouldn't think we were doing what she said. Robbie climbed in his window. I went around to the front to go in, but something stopped me when I put my hand on the doorknob. I had the quilt me and Robbie had to sit on out back. I wrapped it around me and slept all night out on the porch swing.

It was grayish and foggy, not quite light when I woke up next morning. Mama was in the rocker beside me, wrapped up in her old shawl and looking out toward the river. When I sat up a little she got up and went inside. I figured she was mad, but it didn't exactly hurt me. I was out of reach of her being mad. She come back out in a few minutes with a cup of coffee in each hand.

"That'll warm you up," she said and she sat back down in the rocker warming her own hands around her cup. "Linney," she said, never looking up from that cup of coffee. "Wasn't none of this my idea."

"Mama," I said, "that don't help me one bit."

She nodded without looking at me still, like her feelings was hurt, but I was out of reach of that too. She went on in the house and started breakfast. I heard them all in there, moving around and clanking plates and talking. I heard Mama tell Robbie to fix him and me a plate and take them on out to the porch. I sat right up, I was surprised how hungry I was. It was eggs and biscuits and gravy like always, but Mama'd fried up a jar of sausage from last fall and there was something about the chill in the air out on the porch that made it all taste so good. We just finished and set our plates down on the porch floor when Daddy come out. He kissed me on top of my head, then him and Robbie went on out—not to the cornfield but to the field next to it which used to always be beans, but now Daddy is thinking about all them railroad men and miners and tobacco. This is working out for Daddy, I thought.

After a bit Betts come out to fill up the dishpan at the pump and made a face at me on her way back in. I didn't know what Mama was doing, seemed like she was having an ordinary day in the house. Seemed like everybody was having an ordinary day. Then long

about dinnertime, here come Virgil and Pearl around
the bend in their wagon.

Ordinary Days

March — May 1910

THE THING ABOUT CHOOSING IS, no matter how big the choice you're making, a lot of it happens a penny's worth at a time. Robbie was right about how tired it makes you to be doing other people's things in other people's ways. It didn't leave much fire in you for thinking about choosing. The first few weeks at Chandler's, I'd be so tired by suppertime I couldn't hardly chew. I was already that tired by the time we got there that first night. Virgil and Pearl had figured to spend the night with us the day they came for me because it was way too late to head back and anyway, they wanted to see Robbie.

I tell you what, I would not want to do that again. I wisht I'd had a little time between what I figured out about choosing, and them showing up. I mean, I just had that morning when I woke up out on the porch to feel a little free. I didn't get to where I was strong in it before they was there to get me.

That night, through supper and after, Virgil and Pearl, they only had eyes for Robbie, though every once in a while I seen Pearl looking at me in a way I wasn't used to being looked at. I didn't even know what to call it till I went to bed and thought about it. It was a part of it sad, for I think she was also seeing Robbie when she was looking at me. But there was something else too.

She looked interested.

Mama and Daddy, on the other hand, kept their eyes everywhere but on me, I guess I should have known it would be like that. Daddy bragged on Robbie's working to Virgil and they talked farming and money and what they called the prospects of tobacco. Mama and Pearl went off in a corner or in the kitchen by themselves a couple times and talked where nobody could hear them. I stuck by Robbie much as I could, but his Mama and Daddy were mostly keeping him close. Almost every time I looked for him, though, he already was looking back at me. Betts I'm sure was there, but I don't actually remember seeing her till it was time to go to bed. Me and her slept on pallets out in the front room so Virgil and Pearl could have our beds. I didn't care about that. It already wasn't my bed.

Come morning, Mama and Pearl made up breakfast and a dinner basket for me and Virgil and Pearl, and everybody ate fast and nobody talked. I couldn't eat much more than a biscuit. I didn't even feel real. My head had gone all cottony and all that food on the table, seemed like there was some kind of spell on it, like it might turn me to stone if I tried to eat it. Then we were all walking out to the wagon and I don't remember having a thought in my head except for being surprised when Pearl got into the back with me.

From the start, I got up when I heard Pearl moving around, to help her with breakfast. That first morning when I woke up, I couldn't feel my hands and feet. I knew I had to get up out of the bed, get dressed, and walk out of the room—but there wasn't no part of my body willing to believe it was so. I didn't even know where to stand when I got into the kitchen. Their kitchen is in the front of the house, which faces east like ours but with no mountain close by, so it gets the morning sun. I couldn't hardly believe how nice that made the kitchen feel.

Pearl was standing at a long table set under the window with her back to me, mixing up biscuits. She didn't hear me come in so I stood there a minute, looking. She's shorter than me, and softer looking than me and Mama in her body, almost like she's got pillows inside her dress. I knew her dress and apron both was done up from feedsacks, for I had nightgowns made up from both them patterns—her dress was printed with long curvy falling leaves in brown and green and pink, and her apron was navy blue with white polka dots. Mama makes up our nightgowns and aprons from feedsacks, but we generally buy cloth for our dresses in Paintsville. Pearl's hair was in a knot at the back of her neck like Mama always tries for, but it was a nubby little twist and it had a lot more gray in it than Mama's. I hadn't thought about Virgil and Pearl being older than Mama and Daddy, but me and Robbie were about the same and he was their next-to-least while I was Mama and Daddy's oldest. I opened my mouth to say Good morning, but then I closed it.

I was trying to think what Robbie called Mama and Daddy but I couldn't remember him calling them anything at all except for his Yessirs and No thank you ma'ams. We wasn't brought up to call grownups by their first names, so I didn't know. I felt my shoulders sag with how hard it all felt just then, but then I stood back up straight. Maybe I wasn't a grownup, but I wasn't a child neither. And if I was going to live there, I had to know what to call them.

I put my bad hand behind my back. Then I put my good hand behind my back too and held onto it. Then I brought them both out in front and covered up my bad hand a little with my good one across my middle.

"Good morning," I said.

"Well, good morning, honey," she said, turning halfway around. "You're just in time to crack eggs for me."

You would think I might not be good at cracking eggs, but I'm pretty fast at it since I can pick one up with my good hand, crack it on the edge of a bowl and set the shells off to the side all without changing hands. I set into doing it.

"Well, now," she said. "Isn't that something." She took the bowl from me, scrambled up the eggs real quick and poured them into a hot skillet just starting to smoke with bacon grease on the stove. There was coffee making too. It smelled good in there.

She handed the empty bowl back to me and I held it under the edge of the table with my good hand and raked the broken shells—a couple dozen's about right for breakfast, she'd said—into it with my bad hand. I swallowed and kept my eyes on the broken shells in the bowl.

"I can crack them pretty good," I said. "But I'm not so good for gathering. I can't lift the hens up quick enough with my bad hand to snatch the eggs out with my good one. They get me about every time, I almost always come out bleeding."

"We can't have that," she said. "Walty gathers for me, he can keep on, it won't hurt him a bit."

I took that in.

I straightened up with the bowlful of broken eggshells crooked in my right arm. I couldn't quite look at her.

"I don't know what to call you," I said.

She looked up then from what she was doing, cutting out rounds of biscuit dough with a glass. She stood there a minute with one hand still flat on the patted-out dough and the other hand dangling that floury-lipped glass. She looked at me, looked at all of me, kind of head to foot. It was that interested look again.

"Pearl," she said. "Pearl will be just fine."

And that was my first penny's worth of choosing.

I would ask when I didn't know. I would say what hurt me.

I barely had time to think that thought when I heard a ruckus somewhere through the house. A tabby cat run squalling and slipping and sliding into the kitchen and right behind her an old woman with a straw broom. I got quick out of the way, backing up flat as I could against the worktable.

"Damn stinking cat," she kept saying, and all the while she's whacking that broom down around on the floor like the cat's still there, which it sure ain't, cats being smart as they are—it'd jumped up on the worktable into the leavings of the biscuit dough and on out the window. Then she bent over from the waist and started poking with the broom underneath everything in the room there was to poke under, saying things to that cat I couldn't quite make out. She stood up, holding the broomstick in one hand down at her side, level, like a man holds a shotgun. "Damn thing pissed on my rug" she said to Pearl. Then she seen me. "Cover your eyes if you need to, girl," she said. "I'm about to kill me a cat."

I almost wanted to laugh, not a mean laugh, but the kind that happens to a little kid when they see something they've never seen before, say like the first time they see a jack-in-the-box pop out and it's as good a chance they'll cry as laugh. Pearl wasn't looking like laughing. I snatched up the glass she'd been using and shoved the bowl full of eggshells toward the back of the table against the wall where it couldn't get swiped off by the broom. Pearl wiped her hands on her apron and took a few steps closer to Aunt Hesty, to where she could grab hold of the broom without getting all the way in range of it.

"Ain't no cats dying today, Mommy," she said. "Didn't I tell you not to shut her in there with you all night?"

"Oh, be quiet, Pearl," she said. She was looking at me then, lifting her chin up a little, like somebody who thinks you're fixing to cheat them if you can. She worked her mouth around, how old people sometimes do when they're thinking, then she poked me with one finger in the middle of my chest and said, "You there, girl—what are you doing here?"

It struck me how little I'd thought about Aunt Hesty while I was waiting to come here. I hadn't made any kind of picture in my head about her, which is just as well for nothing I'd have imagined would have fit. She's shorter than me, shorter even than Pearl. She's about the same size in her body as Pearl, but she's not got that softness. She's wide across, kind of flat when you look at her from the side, and bony, her body's got a knobby look to it. And crooked. Like one shoulder or a rib or hip's been pulled out of line, so that when she walks even her elbows and wrists are working, even her chin and jawbone's in on it. She's got what Mama calls salt and pepper hair, real springy, but she don't do it up in a knot, she makes a long skinny braid that hangs down her back all the way to where her apron's tied at her waist. Her face is wrinkled the way a man's will be when he's worked all his days out in the sun. She's fair, though, and her eyes are regular blue with a deep blue ring around and she's still got dark thickish eyebrows that peak just past the center of her eyes so she always looks like she's paying attention.

I had to think a long time about her eyes before I had a word for them. Alarming. If she looks at you straight on, alarming is the word. Mostly, though, she looks at things sidewise, out the corner of her eye.

"Linney's Rose and Carl's eldest girl, Mommy. Come to help me for a while," Pearl said. She was bent over, putting the biscuit pan into the oven. I was glad she spoke, for I didn't have an answer on the tip of my tongue—if Aunt Hesty was asking, she didn't know I was there to watch on her. Pearl had put the broom over in the corner out of reach but still, I didn't want to start nothing.

"Well, you need it," Aunt Hesty said, turning around to the stove. "You're about to burn up these eggs." She started to reach for the handle of the skillet with her bare hand, but Pearl got there first with a towel wrapped around her hand for picking up the smoking skillet, one eye on me to make sure I was seeing what was happening. Aunt Hesty huffed at her and rolled her eyes at me to make sure I understood how Pearl was behaving. Then she inched over and got her broom back and cracked Pearl across the top of the head with the handle.

"Holy...." I thought, then slapped my good hand up over my mouth as if I'd said it out loud. I couldn't believe I even thought it out loud, I'd only heard Daddy say it once or twice.

Pearl grabbed the broom back and stood froze and hunched over for a just a second, like somebody waiting for a bad stomach cramp to pass. She put the broom back in the corner, set Aunt Hesty down to the table and nodded at me to sit down beside her. Then she went back to the worktable, dishing up what eggs weren't burnt onto the bottom of the pan. I got a quick thought of how mad Betts would be to have to wash a skillet like that, but then Virgil and the boys started coming in. I still didn't have them straight, they looked all different sizes and shapes to me, a couple of them dressed and talking, a couple still looking half asleep and their hair sticking up every which way.

"Morning, boys," Pearl said, and she put the eggs and a big pitcher of milk in the middle of the table. "Get started on the eggs, biscuits'll be a minute."

April 6, 1910

Dear Robbie,

It is Sunday afternoon and I am writing to you out on the back porch, which is as close as I can get to feeling like us sitting out behind our house after supper. I see what you mean about your farm being so pretty—the dogwood and redbud is coming on up the hills and there is that new green everywhere except where your daddy and the boys has turned the fields. They are out there working now—your mama fussed a little, but your daddy says there's no days of rest for farmers. I figure you've heard that before. I expect you're hearing it still—I know how Daddy is when he's wanting to make something happen.

Anyway, it is after Bible story and after dinner

and Aunt Hesty is taking a nap. Your mama says I am not a farmer, so she will listen for Aunt Hesty to wake up and they'll work on their quilt they're making and I can sit out here and catch my wits, as your mama says. She knows I am writing you a letter. She says, Tell my boy I love him and I miss his face.

I miss you too, Robbie. Especially I feel it when we sit down to the table. I imagine you here and I imagine you there, and it feels like you are nowhere and me neither. Then I feel like I'd give just about anything to be sitting at my own, old table, or just to have anything at all be the way it was—even with how it was.

One night I dreamt I was here in your house and all of the sudden I knew it was so wrong and I had to get out and get home, and then all of a sudden again I knew going home was the worst thing I could do, it was some kind of trap. Right at the end of the dream I was standing in a doorway with a tiny little dogwood planted beside it and I couldn't even tell which house I belonged to. When I woke up in bed, first thing I seen was my quilt Mama sent with me and I still didn't know for sure where I was or if I was really awake. Are you having any kind of dreams like that?

Maybe it's a good thing most days I don't get much chance to sit down and let it all come over me. Does it help you to be working all day? Most days I am moving from the time I get up till the time Aunt Hesty goes to bed. I help your mama get breakfast on the table, or else I keep Aunt Hesty out of her way while she cooks. It ain't every day Aunt Hesty needs watched, some days she gets up and helps and *it's all ordinary as can be. She even sings, I think her voice is real pretty, deeper than you'd think for as little as she is. One morning she started singing "Jesus Loves Me." Only she sang "Jesus loves me, He don't know..." then she left off the words and went on to just humming it. I said, "Aunt Hesty, what don't he know?" And she said, "Honey, if I didn't tell him, I sure as hell ain't telling you."*

I busted out laughing and couldn't stop, and she laughed too and hummed even louder, looking at me with I-know-something-you-don't-know eyes and bobbing her head with every note like it was a word, till your mama swatted us both on the rear end with a dish towel and when your daddy and Tom come in we was all three of us bent over and wiping our eyes with our aprons from laughing so hard. Your daddy says, and he's pretending to be all stern and frowny, but he's smiling around the corners of his mouth, he says, "What is going on in here?" Your mama throws up her hands and she can't hardly get it out, she says, "We don't know!" Which set us all off again, even your daddy and Tom, who didn't have a clue as to what it was all about. I tell you what, that was some morning. I never knew ordinary could feel so good. It was like me and your mama and your mamaw, like we was the beginning and the middle and end of some big story, bigger than us, but still all ours.

Then there is the other days when she's all testy and don't care what she says, and it's making her mad that I'm following her around everywhere. She told your mama, with me standing right there with them in the front room, to send me home—"this rabbity girl," she called me—and get you back. I don't even know what that means, Robbie, but she said it so ugly-like. I had to bite down on my lip real hard so as not to cry, for I had begun to think she liked me. That was just a couple of days ago. But your mama come to my room that night and told me some things Aunt Hesty had said to her, so I'd know that on those days, what she says—well, it's not that she don't mean them when she's saying them, it's more like when she's saying them she's not who she means to be. That put me on edge a bit, because Mama was always telling me Betts didn't mean things she said to me when I knew good and well she did—and worse things, that Mama never even heard her say.

"Try and remember," your mama said, and I couldn't tell you if she was about to laugh or to cry, "what 'We don't know.'" I felt some better then. I can't take somebody telling me that what I know ain't so, but I maybe can take some not-knowing even when it comes with hard knocks.

I'm getting along fine with everybody else, the boys is pretty much like you told me. I call Walty Walt like you said, and everything he says to me is so polite, I think it is his version of being a grownup. "Could I pass you the milk, Linney?" or "Could I carry that basket for you?" he'll say, like he's seeing to it I get everything I need. That is a very nice thing. I never told you how surprised I was, that time you said your mama would feel better with another lady in the house. Nobody ever called me that before. Your daddy and all of the boys are working real hard, real long days so we don't see them in the house much except at the table. Every once in a while, though, your daddy stops and tells me to let him know if I need anything and they all look at me and nod their heads like yes, that's right, let us know. Everybody wants to know how you're doing, and they say to tell you they want to hear about our farm, too, what all you and Daddy are doing and how's it going with the tobacco and such as that. I ain't hardly got around to knowing about such things here, I've been so much in the house or else walking around down by the creek with Aunt Hesty.

The hardest part is not having you after supper to tell about how strange it all feels. How there's things from home I don't miss at all. Like Betts. I said that to Mama once when Betts was throwing a fit about something or other, I said, "Well, I won't be missing that." "Oh, you'll miss her," Mama said, "just you give it a bit of time and you will." But I knew I wouldn't. And I don't.

Before I got here and got settled in, I was all set to be mad at your mama like I was at mine. I was carrying this picture from a story book in my head, one of them fairy tale mothers in raggedy clothes standing in the doorway of a hut, stretching one arm out and pointing one finger out toward the wild woods and sending her boy and girl out into the dark. But the more I'm around your mama, the more I like her and the more I can't figure how Virgil got her to say yes to all this. Does all still feel so strange to you too? Write me when you can, Robbie, and tell me whatever you want. I'm waiting to hear.

yr. loving sister,

Linney

If you walked not even a quarter mile out the back door of Chandler's house, down between the cornfield and the barn, and past the apple trees, you'd come on a bit of woods growed up around Hargus Creek. It's a pretty woods, ordinary trees and brush, nothing too hard to get through. There's a big, big rock, big as a room almost, that juts out over a blue hole in the creek. It's darkish out there, just enough sun gets through to speckle the rock long about dinnertime. The boys liked to swim there, but me and Aunt Hesty'd go out there a lot too. You'd think she couldn't get up there, but the rock come out of the ground real slow and leveled off where it hung out over the creek. We might be pumping water, or scouring out pots, or hanging clothes and out of the blue, she'd say, "I need to sit on a rock" and that's what we'd do.

She likes rocks. When we're out walking, if she finds a pretty one or one that looks like a heart or a fist or any old thing, she puts them in her pockets and adds them to a pile she keeps in a corner of her room. Pearl says it does no harm and Aunt Hesty says they're presents, for her boys, she says. "How do you know they're presents?" I asked her once and she stopped in her tracks and stared at me. "What else, young woman, shows up out of the blue in the middle of the road and offers itself up like that?" she told me, shaking her head at me like she didn't know what this world was coming to. Anyway, that's what the days were like— working with Pearl in the house or out in the kitchen garden for as long as Aunt Hesty would last, till she'd take off and I'd have to go running after. I felt bad to leave Pearl with all the work, but some days, when

Aunt Hesty wasn't moving too fast or trying to lose me, I couldn't help noticing how free it felt to take a notion and just run off and follow it.

"Oh, that feels good," I said when we were up on the rock, middle of a morning. We'd been hoeing weeds in the kitchen garden almost since daylight and my back was tired of being hunched over. "I'm so tired, I think I could fall sleep right on this rock."

Aunt Hesty was looking at me pretty close. I was all stretched out on the rock, laying on my back with my arms up over my head and pointing my toes. "You ought not to reach your arms over your head like that," she said. "The cord'll get twisted around the baby's neck and strangle it."

I sat up so fast I didn't even know I was doing it. She scooted back away from me a little, like I'd scared her, but then she said, "Now, Linney, don't think I don't know why your mama sent you up here. Why else would she? It's what they do, it's what they done to me."

"No," I said, shaking my head and my hands and everything on my body that could shake itself no. "No, no, no, no, no." But it was too late. I could see by her eyes she was off somewhere else. She was looking at me, but it was a story in her eyes and it was coming out. I wasn't sure I ought to hear it, but there was not a thing in this world I could do about it.

"I was a Lively," she said. "My daddy was a judge in Lee County, Virginia, way down at the bottom, and all the way west. He was a judge, but we weren't fancy, no, Lee County was mostly just farms, like around here. But we were pretty girls, me and my sister, and that was enough to make us feel a little bit fancy. You got a sister, ain't you?" I nodded.

"I was born on the third day of 1844, so I was, let's see, I was a bit older than you when the War started. And we didn't know, we didn't have no idea about what was going to happen. Well, there was this young man. Robert. Robert Allen Clark. Our daddies knew each other, so I'd known him about all my life, and I was sweet on him ever since I can remember. Now, when he got to be seventeen or eighteen or so, and started looking like a man, Lord, have mercy on my soul. Oh, I loved him, sure as I was a girl. I remember standing in our front room and seeing him come in with all the rest of them Clarks around Christmas time, snow on his hair and them warm, warm brown eyes all lit up and looking all around the room for me before he even got through the door. Tall and smiling, his manliness all shiny and new on him. Standing there looking at him, I swore to myself, 'I will never forget this. I will never not believe it.' For my mama had seen how it was and she was talking at me all the time about young love and how it ain't real. He stood by me when we all made a circle around the Christmas tree and put his hand on my back where nobody could see. Then he let it slide down, and Sweet Angels of Mercy and Grace, it was a Christmas miracle my skirt didn't catch on fire. After that, every time he looked at me it just turned me inside out. You know what I mean."

I did not, but I knew enough to be getting worried about what was coming next. "Maybe we should head back and see if we can help Pearl with dinner," I said, but Aunt Hesty didn't show no signs of hearing me.

"Robert told me that night he was going to ask my daddy if he could call on me, and I told him, I said, 'Don't, for then they'll never give us a moment alone'—and you know what I'm talking about. Even so, I didn't see him much and hardly ever without people around. Every once in a while we could get a walk by ourselves down by the creek, but we never did know for sure if we was alone. Word come down about the War, and he come by himself the very next afternoon, knocking on our door, and asking to speak to Daddy. They went in the front room and closed the door. It wasn't a time for asking to court, he wanted to marry. Daddy said no, not then, but if Robert wanted to marry me when he got back, Daddy would give his blessing for that. I was too young to be widowed, if Robert loved me, he would wait, Daddy said. Then they brought me and Mama into the room and told us what they'd settled. Robbie stayed on to supper and they gave me permission to walk him to the edge of our farm, but I had to be back in twenty minutes, Daddy said. Robert gave me his arm. It was early May, and the sun was low, turning everything gold, and the air was moving all around us, robins starting to sing the sun down. We walked past the barn to the other side of the corn crib away from the house to where there was a patch of high weeds—some dry as straw from last season, some new green shoots coming through—and fell down. That was all it took. And that was Pearl."

She went quiet then, and I sure couldn't think what to say, so we sat there for a few minutes while I looked up the creek at the new green on the trees. The sun was starting to come through and heat up the rock and I figured it must really be getting close to dinnertime. I was trying to figure out what to say to get us moving toward home when she started up again. She'd been stretched out with her legs out in front of her crossed at the ankles, leaning back on her elbows. I didn't know how she was doing it. I had to keep shifting all around to try and stay comfortable on that rock, but seemed like she was back in another body, the body of that girl in love. I never felt that kind of thing my ownself, but I could feel the sweetness of it coming off her. She sat up and bent her legs at the knees, her feet off to one side of her and her bracing herself on the opposite arm held straight and stiff like a prop. Her other arm was down at her side, the palm of her hand flat and down low on her belly.

"Wasn't nobody getting fat in those days," she said "and I was just a little thing anyway. Robert hadn't been gone all that long before you could tell—my sister seen it first and told Mama. The War was bad by then, and getting closer. Mama wasn't wanting my brother Will to go, he was just a little younger than me but they were going that young, all of them was going, and she wasn't wanting him to go. So once all the crying was over, her and Daddy they worked out a plan. There was some land up in Kentucky had been deeded to some great uncle or other up the line that fought in the War of 1812 and they got him to let us settle it. That is this place, Hargus Creek, where we're sitting right now. Me and Will was to come up here together, so both of us could get away. Mama give me a little silver ring that didn't look like a wedding ring but it was wartime so it would pass for one, she said. We was to tell everybody my husband was kilt and I'd come up with my brother to have my baby away from the war. 'I ain't doing that,' I said. 'I'll say he's in the war, but I won't say he's kilt.' 'You'll do as you're told,' Daddy said. But I never did.

It didn't matter whether I did or I didn't, just after Pearl was born, they sent a letter to me and Will up

DIANE GILLIAM

here saying they'd got word he'd been kilt somewhere in Tennessee. Then two years later, another letter that said he wasn't, he'd just got bad hurt and lost and had finally come walking home. And had married my sister a few months later.

I still don't know how that happened, but I never spoke another word to my sister. Don't know if she's still alive and don't care. My brother Will, though, he stayed right with me. He loved Pearl, and he did for her and me and when he married his wife, that was Helen, he told her it would always be that way. We all of us lived here together till he died about ten years ago and they didn't have no children so she went back to live with her own people. She was alright, but generally speaking Linney, I got no use for sisters. I was awful glad when Pearl's boys come along how they did."

I'd been sitting facing her, my back to where the rock drops off over the creek, my legs out in front me like she'd been sitting before. She leaned forward and grabbed a hold of the toe of my shoe and give it a squeeze between her fingers and her palm.

"Get you a brother, Linney, is what I say." She kept those eyes of hers right on my face till I looked back at her.

"Yes, ma'am," I said. I had those pictures in my head of Robbie sitting at our table and pushing back his plate when he was all done, and of his face in the window frame, how he'd dropped his hand down onto my shoulder that first night after they'd told me.

"And get me off this rock," she said, turning over onto her hands and knees, fixing to stand up. "I don't know what you were thinking, letting me sit up here getting all twisted up, now it's going to take me all day to get back straight."

56

"Me, too," I thought. I knew what people would say about a story like Aunt Hesty's. It wasn't a story you'd tell around, and some parts of it, I was pretty sure, you wouldn't be saying out loud to nobody.

I didn't know why she told me all that, but I never thought for a minute she didn't mean to do it.

I wasn't sure what it was just happened between us. It felt like church.

The thing about that morning was, I couldn't get over it. And it wasn't what you'd think. It wasn't what all she told me—though that was a lot. It was something about how she reached out and grabbed my foot when she said that thing about getting a brother. Seemed like when she did that, she knew everything in the world there was to know about me and what I needed. Over the next few weeks, every time my foot remembered what her fingers felt like closing around my toes, I'd look over at her doing whatever ordinary thing she was doing and remember Robbie saying she knew things about people's lives and the turns they took. I begun to believe she did.

A couple of times at night in my room before bed, I got out my pencil and paper and tried to draw bits and pieces of us sitting out on the rock. That's when I realized I hadn't hardly looked at her face the whole time she was talking. When I went to draw, what come out was the crumbly curve of the edge of the rock and the creek winding back from it, under leafed out trees shaped like arms held up for the arch of a Virginia reel. When I tried to draw her hand on my foot, what come out was the roots of a willow showing through a creek bank, and the branches trailing in the water right in front of the roots.

They looked to me more like pictures from a fairy tale book than what my eyes actually seen. I knew they were true pictures, though. I didn't know what any of it meant.

It was getting on towards the end of April, I'd been at Chandlers' about a month. I hadn't paid much attention to the boys before that morning on the rock, but afterwards I begun to look at them different. I seen how close Tom watched Virgil and followed how he talked and acted towards the younger ones. He even held his coffee cup in both hands like it was a bowl and leaned back in his chair to drink it like his daddy did. I seen it rankled Danny and Doug for Tom to tell them what to do when it come to chores and work out in the fields, but they went along. When they was all walking out the door to work, they'd follow Virgil and Tom, aping how they'd swing their arms and scratch the back of their necks as they walked ahead still figuring out the work of the day. Walt would follow after, watching everything, till he veered off to the barn to do whatever chores there was to do out there or whatever Pearl needed done before going on out to help with what he called the real work. They all come in together at dinnertime though, ready to sit and eat and gather theirselves to go back out and do it all some more. Every day just before Virgil pushed back from the table, which was everybody's signal to get up and head back out, he'd lean forward to Pearl and say, "Pearl, honey, you need anything?" And Pearl would say, "Have one of the boys carry us some wash water" or "We're a little low on stove wood" or "No, honey, we don't need a thing." Then he'd wink at her and say, "Well, then" and nod at whichever of the boys was to see to what she needed. Even after supper, Virgil and the boys would go back out and stay as long as there was light, there was no end of work to be done that early in the season.

I worked long and hard too. Every minute of the day when I wasn't following off after Aunt Hesty, I was helping Pearl in the kitchen or the garden. But it felt different. Back home Betts was always squirming things around to get out of work, which meant I ended up doing it. When it was like that, work just made me feel like I was being took for a fool. At Chandler's everybody worked as hard as a body could work—and it was hard—but it didn't suck the life out of you the way it did being mad all the time.

All the while I was watching the boys, I was seeing a ghost of Robbie there with them. I figured him to be filing out in the morning after Danny and Doug, and before Walt. Not really watching anybody else, just getting ready in hisself to do what needed done. I missed him most between supper and bedtime. If the boys was still out working, me and Pearl and Aunt Hesty would be together doing whatever might make the next day easier. Sometimes they'd peel a big bunch of potatoes and set them in a pan of cold water to be ready for the next day, or I'd bring in stove wood for breakfast, or we'd just be washing up dishes and sweeping, gathering up clothes for washing, such as that. Pearl was good to talk, her and Aunt Hesty could talk about a lot of things they remembered together.

They'd bring me in, asking me how my mama did things and what I liked, but at the end of the day, with me still feeling so much from how new it all was, it was Robbie I needed to tell things to. Sunday mornings, Pearl would read a story from the Bible to everybody before they went on to work. When it was Jesus telling a story that people was to learn something from, he'd say something at the beginning and the end of the story like, "He who has ears to hear, let him hear." That was how it was with me and Robbie. Who else would have ears to hear how it was for us?

We were cleaning up after breakfast one morning, me and Pearl and Aunt Hesty, when a man I never seen before come riding up into the yard. Pearl seen him from the window.

"Well, there's Al Marcus," she said, shaking dishwater off her hands and then wiping them off on her apron. "I wonder what he's doing here." We all three of us got out onto the front porch as he was climbing down off his horse. Soon as he turned, he held up his hand and twisted it back and forth—it was two letters he was holding up for us to see.

"I'm just on my way home from Paintsville," he said. "I asked at the Post Office was there mail for anybody up our way and they give me these to bring you." He turned them around and looked at what was wrote on them. "From Robbie," he said. "One's got your name on it, Pearl." He looked at the other one. "Who's Linney?" he asked.

"This is our Linney," Pearl said. Our Linney. She put her hand on my shoulder and pushed me forward just a little. "She's come to help me out. Come on in, now, Al," she said. "The boys are all out working, but there's plenty of coffee and breakfast still and we'll get you all filled up before you head up the road."

He was in a hurry to get home, so he didn't sit too long, which was good because I was itching to get to my letter and I figured Pearl was too. She kept looking at them sitting on the edge of the table while Mr. Marcus had his coffee and answered questions about his wife and girls and told what all he heard while he was in Paintsville. Aunt Hesty started into tapping her foot like she does when somebody's taking too long at anything, and I seen Pearl reach over under the table and put her hand on her leg to stop her doing it. He wasn't wanting to take the time to go out and talk to Virgil, but he told Pearl a bunch of things to pass on to him. A lot of it was about the new railroad coming in, seemed like it was really going to happen this time. He said a lot of numbers I forgot quick as he said them, about prices for crops that ought to go up and wages for railroad work. But Pearl said she'd remember and tell Virgil, and finally Mr. Marcus was up on his horse and heading out.

It was washday, was the thing. With all the spring mud and how hard they were all working, it had been taking us morning till night on washdays to keep the boys in clothes that, if they didn't exactly get all the way clean, was at least wearable. When we got back inside from seeing Mr. Marcus off, I looked at Pearl, and we both looked at letters. I knew we were both thinking we ought at least to get some water on to boil before we opened our letters, maybe even set the first bunch of clothes to soak and get the second kettle of wash water on to boil. I kept my eye on Pearl, and pretending like I was sneaking, I snaked my hand across the table and picked up my letter. She pretended like she was frowning, but reached out real slow and got hers, then we both laughed—you just wouldn't believe how funny we thought we were, times like that. Her and Aunt Hesty went and pulled their chairs together in the front room and I went out onto the back porch. I heard Pearl's voice reading Robbie's words out loud to Aunt Hesty as I unfolded mine, but then I didn't hear nobody but Robbie.

May 1, 1910

~~Dear Linney,~~
~~I hope my letter finds you well.~~

Dear Linney,
I wanted to write you a good letter even though you told me good don't matter, so I asked your mama how to start out and she told me, "Start out—I hope my letter finds you well." But then I couldn't think of any sentences of my own that could follow after that, so I am starting over. Everybody else is asleep. We been getting up with the birds and working till the light's gone and mostly going straight to bed after that. I am tired about all the time but working covers up a lot of the homesick so I guess it's just as well, like you said, to keep moving. But the homesick is there. Sometimes I'll be working along, and I see or smell something— tonight it's the frogs down by the river making such a racket, like they do back home on the creek, that you can't hardly hear yourself think—and my heart and my stomach just turns to clay. I remember all of a sudden that I forgot to go home. It's like your dream, Linney, only it happens to me when I'm awake. I look around me and for a second I think "Well, this ain't right," and I think to set down whatever I've got in my hand and start walking home. Then I remember it ain't right, but it's real. If I could have it however I wanted, I'd be home walking into the kitchen with Daddy and Tom and coming on you and Mama and Aunt Hesty laughing about what Jesus don't know, and having that ordinary morning.
An ordinary morning here these days is one big pot of fuss. When I was a little boy, we had a neighbor, lived on the Marcus place before they came, would

come over ever once in a while when it wasn't a day you could work and play cards with Daddy. When him and Daddy was done playing, before he picked up all his cards and took them back home, he'd build me a house of cards there on the table. He'd make a triangle shape, like a gabled roof and what he'd do is, he'd lay three cards down flat in a row then put two more standing up in the two little gaps between the three cards, leaning them in so they touched each other just at the very top to make that gable shape. I was so sure I could do it and he let me try, but I didn't pay any attention to them three cards on the bottom so when I tried to make them other two into a triangle, they just fell down, over and over.

That's what your mama and Betts are like without you here, they got nothing holding things in place, they're just so mad at each other all the time you hate to be in the room with them. One day we come in at dinnertime and there was food but the table wasn't set. Your mama'd told Betts to wash up after breakfast and she said Betts did such a bad job she put the dishes all back in the dishpan and told her to do them again. Betts run off hollering and stayed off sulking, but your mama was set on her doing it and doing it right so at dinnertime all the dishes was still in the dishpan. Me and your daddy ate everything your mama'd made for dinner in biscuits instead of on plates. I couldn't believe it. I don't know how your Daddy even ate, his jaw was so clenched up. He didn't say nothing about it, at least not right then, for your mama looked fit to bust.

I tell you what, any of us did like that, Daddy'd have us sorry and digging or chopping or mucking in two seconds flat. "Disappointed in you, son," he'd say, and you'd do anything he wanted for long as he said to do it, to get that look off his face. Cause you'd know he was right. That's how it is with us. Not here, though. By the time we come in at suppertime, Betts was back and the dishes washed and set on the table—but your mama still looked so mad I wouldn't have bet any money on who finally done those dishes. I sure didn't mind going back out to work that day, I can tell you that.

I never seen nobody work like your daddy. We all work hard at my house, but there is a lot of us to do it. Your daddy is trying to do more than all of us put together. He's about strong enough to do it, I'll give him that but, I don't know, it's almost like he's not there when he's working. Like whatever he's doing, it's already tomorrow or next month or the end of the season and that's all he's got his eyes on. Before I left home, I heard Daddy tell Mama, "Carl is a driven man, always has been," and now I know what that means. I am driven because your daddy is driving me, but I do not want to be driven, Linney. I want to feel what I'm doing.

Now I'm worrying this is not a good letter, but it's too late to start over. Here is some good parts. Your mama likes me, I think. When I seen how it was with her and Betts, I started asking her, before we go back out after dinner, does she need anything. Mostly she doesn't, but she looks at me like she sees me and she'll say "You're a good boy, Robbie." I am getting faster and stronger all the time, Daddy will be surprised when I get back home to see what all I can do.

Some days I wake up before daylight and go down to the river and fish a little. That gives me time

*to feel things.Do you ever feel, Linney, like you're
homesick for yourself? And nobody minds about
that because it's fresh fish for the table. I wisht I
was there with you all, but I am making do.*

yr. loving brother,

Robbie

I read it over one more time, folded the letter up,
smoothed it flat and put it in my apron pocket. I sat
quiet for a few minutes, looking off at the hills and
thinking about him down by the river in the morning.
I felt like I was right beside him and at the same time
alone with myself. It was that quiet that comes when
you know something, but it's too happy or too sad
or too big to say. It felt like leaving him, to get up
and go back in the kitchen. Pearl was standing at the
worktable when I come in, holding onto the edges of it
with her back to me, looking out the kitchen window.

"Here's Linney," Aunt Hesty said to her. She was
standing off to the side like she was giving Pearl some
air, or maybe standing guard.

"Well," Pearl said, but then she didn't have nothing
else in her to say. I went and stood behind her and
put my arms around her waist and my chin on her
shoulder, so I was facing the same way as her, looking
out window. She didn't make no noise, but I felt a sob
roll up through her like a wave. I shifted my head, so
my cheek was down on her shoulder. Aunt Hesty was
looking at me. She nodded.

"Me and Aunt Hesty's going to go out and get the
fire started and the water boiling for the wash," I said.
"It's getting too warm to do it inside, don't you think?
We'll come and get you when we're ready to start."

Pearl let go the edges of the worktable and laid her arms and hands over mine where they was wrapped around her in the front there. She give a squeeze and held on for just a second, then let go.

Aunt Hesty nodded at me again and started gathering up the wash tub and boards and soap and what all we needed for our day of washing. When we got outside, I had to put my hands on my knees and bend over a minute and let out my breath. I never knew a grown person to cry before. Aunt Hesty waited for me, like she'd waited for Pearl. Then she was all business.

The boys had stacked wood for the fire the night before. There was an iron bar with a hook hanging down from its center and held up by two forked bars over the fire pit. Aunt Hesty picked up the big washing kettle and hung its handle on that hook. Between us we filled it with buckets of water from the pump, going back and forth from the pump to the wash kettle with me holding onto one side of the bucket handle with my good hand and her holding onto the other side. It was a pretty morning, new green everywhere, and it felt like it was going to get hot.

Once the kettle was full, I realized we'd have to go in and get fire from the kitchen stove to get the wash fire started, which I hated to do in case Pearl wasn't ready for anybody to see her yet. Aunt Hesty went in for it and when she come back out she said Pearl was sitting out on the back porch anyway. She pulled some pieces of wood out of the pile before she got the fire going.

"We ain't in no hurry for it," she said.

"No, we ain't," I said.

We both of us sat down on the ground amongst the wash tubs and watched the fire take. The birds had quieted down from their morning busyness and every once in a while we could hear Virgil and the boys shouting back and forth to each other. I didn't mind at all we were going to spend the whole day at washing. I looked over at the pile of muddied up pants and shirts to be done—it was only a matter of doing to set them all clean and right and looking like people again once they was pinned up on the line. Mine and Pearl's and Aunt Hesty's clothes was in another pile, for they'd get dirtier and not cleaner if we washed them up in the same water as the boys'.

Scraping sleeves and collars and knees of pants, dress fronts and aprons against wash boards with that old burning soap, made me think about how people are put together, how some of them make more wear and tear at the elbow, some on the knees or on the seat. There's some seams keep coming apart and got to be stitched up over and over again. When you're washing an apron, you see how the cloth gets worn across the belly from standing up against the edge of the table hours on end, day after day. An apron takes on the shape of a woman's front after a few days of wearing. I remembered what Robbie said about Daddy working so hard and fast he didn't even see what he was doing. You couldn't wash an apron without feeling the woman that wore it, leastways I couldn't, leastways not Pearl's.

Aunt Hesty poked me hard in the side.

"Water's boiling," she said. "You fetch Pearl and let's get a move on."

We worked out there all day except when we were cooking or eating, and still we had to bring half a dozen shirts in wet, to hang out in the morning. We couldn't have tried any harder to get it all done, but there's only so much you can set right in a day. We set the basket over in the corner of the kitchen, one sleeve hanging out over the edge, so empty it hurt to look at it.

Aunt Hesty drug a kitchen chair over there and laid that sleeve across her lap and started petting on it. "Poor wing," she said.

"Once upon a time," she said, "there was a girl who had six brothers. She didn't finish the magic shirts on time, and one of the brothers was left behind." She turned on me. "It's on account of you he's gone," she said, her eyes as glittering and mean as any queen in any story. Pearl didn't look at me, just bustled Aunt Hesty up out of her chair started herding her on toward her room, her jabbing her finger at me all the way and spitting garble about stinging nettles and swans and one-armed boys.

The Place

IT WAS A HARD THING, Aunt Hesty turning on me like that. Took me some weeks before I didn't feel scared to look her in the eye, and a little bit longer before my body'd not go all the way still, like a rabbit hiding in the grass, when she come into the room. I'd almost forgot about her thinking I was having a baby. She never did say anything more about it and I never did tell Pearl about that morning. I didn't know how she'd feel about me knowing that whole story, and when I thought about it I couldn't be sure she knew all of it herself. Maybe she growed up thinking her mama was a proper widow, like Aunt Hesty and her brother'd told everybody else. It didn't feel right to me, not the knowing nor the keeping quiet about it, but it wasn't for me to bring it up. I startled back to thinking about it when I woke up one morning feeling like I had a rock pressing down at the bottom of my belly, my whole belly and back aching from it.

Oh, no, I thought. Please not that.

I just laid there for a few minutes, curling up different ways and trying to get more comfortable, hoping it would go away, that I was wrong. It didn't, I wasn't. All those times when I was getting ready to go, and Mama asked was there anything else I needed and I didn't answer—it was monthly cloths neither of us thought of. I got a bad twinge and had to jump up, thinking I would get it on the bed, on the sheets. This was not the first time. It happened once when I was fifteen, and once again right after the first of this year. Mama said it's that way sometimes in the beginning, you miss some months in between before it settles in regular.

Mama told me about it when I started to get bosoms and I wanted it to happen. Seemed like it ought to make a difference. I'd be more like a woman, more like her, so I thought she'd see me better. Seemed like she did, that first day. It had hurt then too, and she let me take it easy. I did sitting-down work and Betts had to wash dishes by herself, but after that nothing much changed about how she treated me. She still lumped me together with Betts and I might as well not even be there when that happens. The other thing was, it was embarrassing. It was hard enough at home. Mama said to leave my cloths in the outhouse and she would get them and wash them, but I must have got an awful look on my face when she said that.

"Well, what do you want to do about it?" she said. "They've got to be washed."

"I have to do it myself," I said. "You tell me how and I'll do it."

Sometimes we've stayed at other people's houses, on the way to Paintsville, or after a church gathering or something like that, and they put all us girls in a room together to sleep. Some girls just take off their dresses, and even all the rest, and get into their nightgowns right in front of each other without turning around or even stopping talking, like it was nothing. I don't know why, but for me it's not nothing. I've got to turn around, I don't like it. About the only time I ever got my way at home was when I got bigger and Betts kept walking into our room when I was getting dressed.

"It's my room, too" she told Mama, and Mama said, "Linney, that's true."

"Mama, she's doing it on purpose because she knows I don't like it. Look at her," I said. She was making that smile at me, so sure, like she already won. "How about this," I said. "If the door is closed, both of us has to knock and wait before we go in. What's wrong with that?"

Nothing was wrong with it and Mama had to say yes. Then when my monthly come, she give me a little basket to put the cloths in and a little wash basin with soap and a cloth over it. I kept it all under my bed and I could carry it up to my clearing when nobody was watching and take care of things. But I didn't have none of that here.

I was standing barefoot by the side of my bed, trying to hold the blood in, my hands shaking when I pulled back the covers to see if I'd made a stain. At least there wasn't that. I twisted around to check on my nightgown. Yes. How was I going to put my nightgown in the wash pile with everything else, right out where anybody could see? How was I even going to get dressed and go out to the kitchen and sit down? I could tell by the light it was full morning and when I thought to think about it, I could smell coffee and breakfast already cooking. I'd been trying to wake up since daylight, but I'd been having one of those long, drawn-out dreams where you think you are awake and up and moving around, till you wake up just enough to know you're not, but you couldn't wake all the way up to save your life, over and over.

There come a loud knock on the door.

"Linney, Linney." It was Aunt Hesty, Pearl must have sent her to get me. "You better get on out here before these boys eat up everything in the house."

"Linney, Linney, Linney, Linney, Linney, Linney, Linney" When I didn't answer straight away, she started saying my name over and over till it started not even sounding like my name. If she didn't cut it out, everybody in the kitchen was going to start wondering what was going on.

"Aunt Hesty" I said real quiet with my mouth right at the doorframe. "Could you just come in here?" I opened the door just enough for her to get in.

"Honey," she said when she seen me standing there shaking and I was starting to cry. I remembered how brave I felt that first morning with Pearl, when I'd told her I wasn't good at gathering eggs.

I said to myself, "I will be a person who can say what makes her bleed." I couldn't say this, though. I wanted words for it, but there wasn't none. I pulled the tail of my gown around enough for her to see. I thought I might break.

Then I broke.

I started crying and I couldn't stop. I wanted Mama, I wanted to be home. I didn't want this, I wanted for nothing to have ever happened to me. I wanted nothing to ever happen to me again. I felt like I was drowning and hot and cold all at the same time, and a knife in my gut slicing me right up the middle.

Somewhere out at my edges, I heard Pearl telling the boys to grab their breakfast and take it on out to the porch to finish. I must have been making a lot of noise. I must have been saving up all that noise and crying, carrying it inside me for a long time and I couldn't stop it from coming out any more than I could stop the bleeding. I was on the floor when Pearl got to me. Aunt Hesty was standing over me, crying, but Pearl got down on the floor behind me and put her arms around me and rocked me side to side. "There, now," she said, over and over. "There, now. We got you. We got you, Linney." I don't know how long that went on, but when the crying started to be over, she sent Aunt Hesty out to the kitchen for a damp towel. We was both still sitting on the floor, and without taking her hand off me, Pearl come around and starting wiping off my face.

"It hurts," I said to Pearl's face, just inches from mine. The words made it out in the last of the crying. It was the best I could do.

Pearl looked up at Aunt Hesty.

"She's lost her baby," Aunt Hesty said. "There's blood." She was staring at Pearl. Her face was terrible.

"No," I said to Pearl when she looked back at me. I sat up a little but she kept one hand on my knee. "She thinks that's why Mama sent me away, but it's not." I felt so tired, and so thirsty. I looked at Pearl's hand on my knee, I looked up and seen she was trying to think what to say. "I know about it, it's not my first time," I choked a little. "I know what to do but I don't have anything."

"Well, now," Pearl said, and bad as I felt, I couldn't help hearing how much she sounded like Robbie when she said those words. There was time in those words, there was time for a person to get herself together a little bit and feel safe while she was doing it. There was arms around you in those words.

"Well, now," Pearl said again, "I expect we know something about what a young woman needs, even if we haven't been young women in quite a while, don't we, Mommy?"

She asked me how I was used to doing things at home and then her and Aunt Hesty went around the house and got what all I needed. She give me the towel for the moment and told me to get back into bed and to don't worry about a thing. "We got you, Linney," she said, just like before, and smoothed my hair back from my face with her hand once I was laying back in the bed. I heard the two of them out in the kitchen and through the house, talking back and forth and scrounging around for what to tear up for the cloths. I heard Pearl tell Aunt Hesty a couple of times that there wasn't no baby, and she'd just say, "I know, honey, I know." She still thought there had been. I was starting to feel sleepy when Pearl come back in with a little basket and basin and set them under the bed for me. She brought a glass of cold water too, a little plate of buttered biscuits and blackberry jam, and a mason jar full of hot water and wrapped up in a towel.

"Curl up around that where it hurts," she said "and it'll help a little. I'll come see about you when it's time for dinner, but you just holler if you want us before."

I didn't want to think about dinner. One reason I try not to cry is, everybody knows. My face stays splotched up red for hours and my eyes will be all burny and swole up for the whole day, even the next morning. But it wasn't like everybody didn't already know. I slept a little after I ate what Pearl brought me, and the warm bottle of water did help with the other. When she knocked on the door at dinnertime, she come in and sat on the bed a minute.

"Now, when I was a girl, me and Mommy we worked out a code. When I was feeling bad like that and needed to sit down or take a day of rest or whatever, I'd tell her I needed a safety pin. So next time you need anything to do with this, you just tell me you need a safety pin and I'll see to it we get off to ourselves for a minute so you can tell me what you need. Would you feel alright about doing it like that, Linney?"

I nodded.

"You think you can come on out for dinner?"

I nodded again. She patted my hand and went on out so I could get dressed. When I got out to the kitchen, everybody was already at the table. They all looked up at me when I come in.

"Feeling better, Linney?" Virgil said. I nodded—it was a nodding kind of a day. "Well, good," he said. "You let us know if you need anything." All the boys was still looking at me and they nodded too.

"I'll settle for a big plate of anything right now," I said. I was hungry and feeling empty and washed out all the way around. I sat down in my place next to Aunt Hesty and they started passing me everything there was on the table. I let them.

"Ladies first," Walt said, and for once Danny and Doug didn't make fun of him.

"Well, now," Pearl said, "that's what I like to hear."

Once we all had our plates full, the talk fell off.

I was too tired and achy to try to make anybody else feel better. I didn't even try. That was my only penny's worth of choice for that day.

I leaned a little against Aunt Hesty, she was quiet too. She'd changed into a black dress, on account of the baby.

That night I dreamed about the doe again. I am back home, up in my clearing with my basket and wash basin, to do my private washing. But I don't have any water in the basin. I have to go back down the hill to the pump, and the hill is so steep, steep like a ladder propped up against the side of a barn. I don't see how I can get down, but I do, there is something rough, almost like steps, cut into the hillside and when I need to I can back down on my hands and knees. When I get ready to go back up, the hillside is straight up and down, there is only something that looks like a rope bridge hanging down off the side of the hill. The boards to walk on are old and splintery with a lot of them missing altogether, and the hand ropes look like a grapevine, two vines about a finger thick twisted around each other, long curly strings coming off them and hanging down. I've got the basin of water in my good hand and I see it's impossible, but I reach out with my bad hand anyway. I take ahold of the vine and I am back up in the clearing.

When I get there, though, the water in the basin is bad, dirt from the fields in it, bits of dead weeds and straw, manure, withered looking corn husks. Some kind of black wormy looking bugs. I throw it away from me. All the mess spills out and I go over and pick up the basin with two fingers and bang it upside down on the ground to get the last bugs out, then turn to go back down the hill again.

It's even steeper than before, only this time there is a fallen tree the whole length of the way, with branches I can grab onto to help me get down, but they are exactly too far apart for me to reach from step to step so I keep sliding and jerking partway awake—that feeling like you're falling—as I'm going back down the hill. When I go to climb back up, this time it's not the bridge, but just a grapevine or maybe a branch of laurel, about as thick as my arm, hanging down loose against the hill for me to climb back up on.

I touch it and I'm in the clearing again, looking down at the basin of water, which is bloody now and there's something floating in it that looks like it's been gutted out of some little animal. Then I remember. Aunt Hesty was right. I did have a baby. I look over at the little cloth covered basket, something is moving in there. Just barely, because I've not fed it nor held it, nor give it water nor nothing for days and days. I fall forward from where I'm sitting, I can't even take the time to stand up and walk over there, that's how close the baby is to dying. The edge of the basket is just in reach of my two longest fingers, and I drag the basket back to where I'm sitting on the ground. I lift the cover.

It's the fawn.

I hear that crackle and snap of a deer stepping through dry woods, and there she is, the doe. She is looking at me like that, like before. Then I am seeing the fawn in the basket, she's only about as big as my hand, I could hold her in one hand, that's how little she is. She's wet, I don't know if it's birth waters or death sweat. She's trembling that tremble animals do when they're so scared they can't run, all they can do is shake. It is awful to see. The doe is looking at me. I don't know if it is her first or her last breath the fawn is trying so hard to take. I am me and the doe and the fawn, all at the same time, and I think, "It's too late, it's too late."

And that's when I woke up. My nightgown was soaked with sweat but I was shivering, and I had to get up and clean myself. When I got back in bed, I didn't have any idea how long till morning and I was afraid to go back to sleep.

"It was just a dream" I said over and over, like I used to say a prayer over and over when I was a bitty girl and scared at night, till I could feel myself starting to fade. "Just a dream, a dream." But I knew it wasn't.

Come morning, I woke up like usual when I heard Pearl out in the kitchen moving around and getting the stove going and the coffee on. I was feeling pretty wrung out, but I didn't want anything to be like yesterday, so I got right up and went out to help. She had a batch of dried apples soaking in a bowl of water on the worktable.

"I thought I'd do us up a pan of fried apples," she said, when I asked what she wanted me to start on. "A little sweetening never hurt a person, is what I'm thinking."

"Mama only does them when we've got fresh," I said. I couldn't take my eyes off them apples. I couldn't think of anything that sounded better than anything sweet. "You'll have to tell me what to do."

She showed me how to lay them out on a towel and press most of the wet out of them.

"Probably everybody does them a little different," Pearl said. "What I do is, get a little bit of butter in the pan, then the apples all cut up into chunks, sprinkle them light all over top with sugar, and when they get hot and soft and start juicing up a little, then I take them off the stove and cover them and let them sit—they cook a little more in the pan, but they don't get too soft that way. And if I've got it, which right now I do, I give them a pinch of cinnamon when I sprinkle on the sugar."

I done just like she said. They smelled so good. How Aunt Hesty said 'Lord have mercy' when she was talking about her Robert—that's how good they smelled. That smell pulled Danny and Doug out of their beds, they showed up in the kitchen even before Virgil and Tom, Walt not too far behind them.

"What are you all sniffing around for," Pearl said to them when they come in and sat down in their places at the table "looking all nosey-faced?" She reached across the table and grabbed Walt's nose between her thumb and forefinger and give it a wiggle. He didn't like that, and Danny laughed and elbowed him when he shoved Pearl's hand away. I pretended I didn't see and figured when I set everything out on the table I'd make sure to set down the skillet of apples in front of his place. "Ladies first," he'd said at the table yesterday when I was feeling so bad.

"Pearl, honey, I believe that was the best batch of fried apples you ever cooked up," Virgil said, when everybody was about done with breakfast. Pearl give him such a pinch on the arm and the boys all laughed—him and Tom had come to the table last and didn't know I did the apples.

It was a good morning. The only thing off about it was Aunt Hesty. She'd come in just before Virgil and Tom and had sat through breakfast without hardly talking. Once Virgil and the boys had gone out to work and we was washing up, I took notice she still had on that black dress and that sent me back to thinking about the fawn in the basket in my dream. If Aunt Hesty knew about thing like signs and what happens when you die, like Robbie said, maybe she knew about dreams.

"Aunt Hesty," I said when Pearl went out in the yard to toss out the old dishwater and get some clean from the pump, "I had a dream."

She looked at me with those eyes. I tried not to look away, but I had to.

"Of course you did," she said. "We can't talk about it here."

Pearl come back in just then with the dishpan. I went back to sweeping under the table. She poured the water into the kettle on the stove to get hot. "Gather me up the coffee cups, Mommy," she said, without really looking at us. Aunt Hesty gathered them up and pushed them together over on the worktable where Pearl had set the dishpan. She looked over at me, then turned back to Pearl.

"I need to walk," she said, not to nobody in particular, how she does when she's fixing to take off.

"Well go on then, you two," Pearl said. "We're almost done here anyway. But you take it easy on Linney, Mommy, you remember she's not quite feeling quite right."

Aunt Hesty looked over at me and lifted one eyebrow, "Oh, I will," she said to Pearl. "Don't you worry about it."

Pearl looked up then, from piling the cups into the dishpan. She threw her dish towel over one shoulder, kind of squared off with Aunt Hesty there by the worktable and put her hands on her hips. "Well, now," she said, giving Aunt Hesty the big eye and giving herself a minute to think about it. "How come all of a sudden I'm feeling just a little bit worried?"

"How should I know?" Aunt Hesty said. "You always was kind of a worrier." She looked at me out of the corner of her eye. "You ain't worried are you, Linney?"

Matter of fact I was. Right then I was feeling pretty worried. If I was a cat I might have jumped right out the window.

"No, ma'am," I said.

"Well, go on, then," Pearl said. "Far be it from me—" But Aunt Hesty was already out the door and down off the porch and there wasn't nothing to be done but for me to take off after her.

She was almost all the way to the woods before I caught up. That was a long way for her to be ahead of me, but I didn't feel like flat out running and I kept her in sight. When she got close to the edge of the woods, I thought I'd have to make a run for it, but she stopped and looked back to see where I was. She paced back and forth there at the edge till I got there.

"I need to sit a minute," I told her. I was sweating and achey and feeling like I could throw up if I didn't catch my breath.

"No, not now," she said. She went right on into the woods and there couldn't be no hanging back for me then. If I lost sight of her in there who knew what it would take for us to find each other again.

"Aunt Hesty," I said, pushing through and holding my arms out like somebody that's been blindfolded, trying not to get slapped by the low branches and saplings that she sent whipping back in her path. "I mean it."

"I know you do," she said, and kept right on going. I couldn't tell where she was headed. She'd have kept on straight if we were going to our rock, and we weren't going straight. She seemed to know where she was going, though—every once in a while she'd slow down, look around, walk over and put her hands on a tree before she took a turn this way or that. Best I could tell, we were walking north. Where the creek bowed out west, the woods got thicker, deeper, and the ground got uneven and harder to walk. I had to concentrate so hard on my footing and on not losing sight of her that we'd gone in pretty deep before I noticed the air under the trees had that dark look of creek water, and the brush and the ground had lost their dapple. We were starting uphill, too. I didn't like it.

She was slowing down, though, and I was almost right behind her when she stopped and stood still, looking upwards and scanning a bit of hillside that was a little clearer than the rest, not too far up. I hadn't noticed how much noise we'd been making, crashing through there, till we stopped and the quiet took over. It was a quiet that came right inside you, like a spell. I come up beside Aunt Hesty so I could see where she was looking and put my arm around her shoulder.

"What are you looking for?" I asked.

"The place," she said. "I think that's it there." She pointed to a long, narrow rock ledge jutting out three or four feet from the hillside, shaped kind of like our rock over the creek if it our rock was upside down. I didn't see it at first, that whole slope of the hill was all piled over with leaf litter from last season.

"Where there's that gap of shadow, but no trees around," she said.

"I see it now," I said. There was something about that quiet that made me not ask any questions. Aunt Hesty stood looking a minute more, then kind of shook herself and started walking. It wasn't far, but it was steep to get up there. She still had her apron on from our morning in the kitchen and I followed behind her holding onto her by the back knot of her apron strings at her waist. I knew she wasn't going to run off from me, but there was something about whatever it was we were doing that made me want to hold onto her. We were both of us out of breath when we got up there. I seen it was the mouth of a little cave. Well, I didn't know if the cave was little. The opening was about four feet high, maybe six or seven feet across. The rock that jutted out from the hillside made like a little roof over that opening, almost like a porch roof. We swept some of the leaf and twig mess clear with our feet and set down on a littler rock ledge just in front of the mouth of the cave. It was all the way dark behind us, that forest dark before us, no real sunlight getting all the way through, but lightened up here and there by the new leaf green of some of the trees that come on late in the spring.

"I come up here after that first letter that said Robert died," Aunt Hesty said. "Will and Helen was new married by then and she'd watch on Pearl while I went walking."

"Yes," I said. I could feel it. I was sitting cross-legged, kind of hunched forward with my elbows on my knees and my hands loose in my lap. I reached out to my sides and laid my palms flat on the rock. It was cold. It was hard. It would hold a person up.

"You hear that?" Aunt Hesty asked.

Out from us, leaves moving at the very treetops when the breeze raked shallow through them. A bird here and there, but they were past their morning busyness. You heard the quiet around them when they called out more than the call. Behind us, coming out of the cave, something like an echo, if the quiet itself could have an echo.

"Yes," I said again.

"It lets the true things come through," Aunt Hesty said. She shifted her weight around, rearranged herself to where she looked a little more comfortable sitting there on the rock. "Same as sleep. Go slow now and tell your dream."

I didn't look at her while I told it, we was both of us facing out toward the trees. Then I went back and told her the other one about the fawn chained by the house, and then about when Robbie come and I remembered the doe when I seen him standing there in the yard watching Pearl and Virgil go.

"What was you hungry for just then?" she asked me.

"When? When Robbie come?"

"When you first seen the doe in the woods, what was you hungering for?" she asked.

"She was the one—"

"No, huh-uh," Aunt Hesty said. "Why was you out in the woods, what happened right before you went out there and seen her?"

I had to let the quiet take me back to where I could remember. Aunt Hesty waited while I sat there looking out through all the tree trunks and leaves and brush, for any of them true things she said would come through.

I was hungry that day. I was fifteen, it was my first monthly, early March. It was almost over, and I was glad because it had got old real quick. And March is hard all by itself. I don't know why it feels colder then than when you've got a hard freeze like in February, but it does. You start to take it personal, how cold it is, and you've been cooped up so long—we was all getting pretty touchy about any little thing. Also, everything in the cellar starts to run out. Mama'd sent me out to the barn to get Daddy for dinner. She had a cornbread on the stove. There was a bowl of cabbage sitting at each of our places at the table. She had cut up the last little piece of ham, fried it up and was laying the pieces on top of the cabbage on our bowls. Hardly any on hers and Daddy's. The rest divided between me and Betts, four or five little pieces about the size of the end of a spoon.

It looked so good. I don't care for cabbage, but I expected I could make it through that big bowl if it had that ham on top. I figured Mama didn't see me there in the front room because I heard her say to Daddy, when we got back from the barn, "Linney's not been feeling good, she won't eat that much." And she took two of them little pieces of ham off the top of my bowl and hid them under the ham in Betts's bowl. I felt like somebody kicked me in the stomach. Then she called us in.

"What did you do?" Aunt Hesty asked.

"I ate what they give me," I said. "Mama said, 'You not feeling good, Linney?' but I wouldn't say yes nor even nod to that, just pretended like I didn't hear her. I got up from the table and put my coat back on and walked down to the river. I always feel more real around rocks and water, Aunt Hesty, I don't know why. I didn't feel real while I was sitting at the table, and none of them felt real to me neither.

But the doe, she come down there looking to drink, and she felt real. When she looked at me, I felt real again. I'd have give her anything I had."

"I know you would," Aunt Hesty said, and she grabbed hold of my knee and give it that same squeeze, how she'd done before to my foot. "Here's the thing,

Linney. She's you, and you're her. There wasn't no asking in her eyes because she already knew everything there was to know about you and what you'd do. Why do you think she brought you her fawn in that dream with the chain? She knew you was the only one could get it to what it needed."

I started to feel dizzy, almost like something was pulling me back into the cave. I wasn't seeing anything around me, only the doe and the fawn and the chain, the dream again. I covered my eyes with my hands and let my body tilt over till I had my head on Aunt Hesty's shoulder.

"That's right," she said. "You'll find your way through better if you cover your eyes. You think you can see everything better in the light, but some things you've got to be in the dark to see. Come on now." She started shifting around to stand up, so I had to get up too. She turned around and bent down to go into the cave.

"Oh, no," I said, and tried to pull my arm back but she'd got a good hold on it. "Aunt Hesty, we can't go in there, we might not get back out."

"Oh, we're going in," she said. "Like it or not."

I couldn't get loose of her and anyway, I couldn't let her disappear into that dark and just stand there waiting to see if she come back out. It was tall enough for us to stand up when we got inside. She didn't go far in, just the length of a house maybe, and you could still see the light at the mouth of the cave from where she stopped. Once my eyes got used to the dark, I seen a little fire ring, some shapeless looking odds and ends on the ground. The ground was a little bumpy, but not too rough, same with the walls and the roof. It smelled like rock and cold air.

"Sit," she said, and I did. She pulled a match out of her apron pocket and lit up the bit of kindling that was inside the fire ring. It wasn't much wood, that made me feel better, like we wouldn't be there for long. I settled myself down a little and looked across the fire to Aunt Hesty. She was staring into the fire. The light from it and the dark all around changed her face. Her edges were softer, her eyes looked deep and glowy. I didn't have any words to say, nothing to ask. Because, what could I ask? Whatever was happening, I didn't know what it was, I couldn't think of a question that wouldn't have made it smaller.

I felt I was behind the eyes of the doe, and whatever happened would happen, it was not for me to say.

"I come here the day the letter come that said Robert was kilt," she said, never taking her eyes off the fire, nor even seeming to blink. "I'd been here before, come and sit outside and gather myself while I was waiting for Pearl to be born, and a few times after, when Helen would watch her for me. See, I only went along with coming up here because I expected him to come back and find out what they'd done and come straight up here for me. He didn't know about Pearl before he left, there wasn't time enough to find out. I was sure I was having a boy baby. I knitted up a little jacket in blue wool, and I had a good bit left so I set in to making a neck scarf for Robert—I had this picture in my head of him holding the baby in the little blue jacket, looking so proud and with his scarf all wrapped around his neck. I brung both them things up here that day and burned them in the fire."

She picked something up off the ground and poked around at the wood. She held it up and turned it all around in her hand, looking at it from every which way.

"The knitting needles, too," she said. "But they was steel so they didn't burn, see? No earthly good to me, though. I couldn't pick them up and make something different, couldn't make any of it come out different. I didn't want nothing different from what I wanted." She looked out toward the mouth of the cave, where it was lighter. "Except for Pearl, of course. Biggest surprise of my life, her coming out a girl." She was holding that knitting needle loose in her fingers, and she begun to tap it on the ground, like somebody who's getting to be in a hurry, but there wasn't no hurry. She looked at me then.

"There is all kinds of borning and all kinds of dying in this world," she said "and in the other one, and in the in-between, and it ain't never over. You think you are one thing, but you are not." She waved the knitting needle back and forth like wagging a finger. Behind her, I seen the fire make the shadow of the needle long as the room itself, it swept back and forth over the whole room of the cave till Aunt Hesty pointed it straight at me.

"The bones of the girl, they go in the fire but they don't burn, they stay the same. But everything else, from the bones out—nothing can stop the borning and the dying. That's what the bleeding is for, so you know, so you don't forget. Are you hearing what I'm telling you, girl?"

I looked at her. Like the doe, like that. I was on the other side, on the inside of that look.

"Good," she said. "I'd hate to think we come all this way for nothing. Now, answer me this." She pointed to the black dress she still had on from yesterday. "What's this for?"

The tears come so sudden, and so true.

"Me," I said. "The fawn."

"Dying or borning?"

All through my body I felt the blood, how it had woke me up and set me shaking, how Pearl rocked me there on the floor and how much it all hurt. I choked. "I don't know. Both."

"Good," she said, and I believed her. She put down the knitting needle and got on her hands and knees to begin the long unfolding that was her way of getting up. "We got to get out of here now, Linney. It don't do to stay too long."

We had to bend down again to get out at the mouth of the cave and when I stood back up I couldn't hardly believe it was still daylight.

"Don't it seem strange out here?" I asked Aunt Hesty.

"That it does," she said. She stood there a minute with her hand shading her eyes, though there wasn't enough sun coming through even to cast a shadow. "We'll be used to it again by the time we get home. Come on, now, we better get a move on before Pearl sends out the cavalry."

Aunt Hesty didn't run on ahead of me on the way home, we walked side by side. We didn't have no sense at all of what time of day it was, as we couldn't see the sun, but we knew Pearl would be worrying. Still, we couldn't neither of us hurry. I give Aunt Hesty my arm over the rough patches, tree roots and rocks and such as that, and she walked along looking down at the brush and telling me this and that about the plants and bushes and trees.

There was a shed snakeskin by the side of the path that made me jump, but she'd seen it on the way in, she said. "Good sign," she said. "New life." Somewhere along the way it begun to rain. We could hear it clattering on the leaves up overhead, but we stayed pretty much dry under that green roof. By the time we could see the edge of the woods beyond the barn, the rain was coming down pretty good. We stopped four or five feet back, still under the cover of the trees. It wasn't just about the rain. I looked at Aunt Hesty.

"It's alright to go back," she said. "You never was just one thing, it's just that now you know it out loud."

I thought how that night Robbie told me it was all a done deal I knew whatever I'd been before, that was done. And how that first morning in the kitchen, I asked Pearl what I needed to ask her and told her what I needed to tell.

Just then, we come up on the edge of the brush, looking toward the house, we seen Pearl come out, pacing and looking out toward where we was. We stepped forward a little so she could see us. I reached for Aunt Hesty's hand and held onto it.

I had broke apart yesterday. I couldn't stop it and I couldn't do a thing to make anybody feel better about it, and I was still alive and still me and different. Pearl was back out on the porch with a couple of big towels, she was waving us in.

I turned and looked Aunt Hesty full in her eyes. "I do know," I said.

"Well, then, honey," she said. "Let go of me and take them young legs of yours and run for it."

I stepped up to the edge of the wood, looked back at Aunt Hesty and breathed in the wet green. I took another step out of the brush, and lifted my face and the palms of my hands for just a second to the rain, and then I shook myself a tiny bit, looked straight ahead and run for it.

Things You Talk About, Things You Don't

June – July 1910

AUNT HESTY WAS WRONG about one thing, I wasn't used to anything by the time we got back home. I was seeing everything through the eyes of the doe, and I was as shaky as the fawn for weeks after coming out of the cave with her. It was like I could see straight inside of things, and everything went straight inside of me, like I'd never before been in this world. I felt skinned. I felt lucky.

We missed dinner the day we walked off into the woods, that's what set Pearl to getting so worried. She was fussing up a storm at Aunt Hesty before we even got all the way in the door. Aunt Hesty kept turning her back to her and trying to shoo her off with her hands, but Pearl just run circles around her, trying to look her in the eye and tell her what all was wrong with her taking off how she did. I knew that kind of trying when I seen it, from trying to make Mama hear what I was saying. Finally Aunt Hesty started taking off her wet clothes right there in the front room. Pearl was trying to wrap a towel around her, but Aunt Hesty put her hands flat on Pearl's chest and pushed her off.

"We're here, ain't we? You're looking at us safe and sound, ain't you? So hush up about it Pearl and fetch me a dress out of my room—or are you fixing to keep me in the house all wrapped up in a towel?" She was on the rag edge of shouting.

Pearl stared at her a minute, then started back toward her, but Aunt Hesty raised her eyebrows and lifted one hand with her forefinger pointing up, the way you warn a child against doing something she already knows better than to do. Pearl threw both her hands up in the air, then slapped them back down on her legs and turned on her heel to get Aunt Hesty her dress without saying another word.

I loved Pearl. If I didn't know it before, I knew it then.

I went on into my room before she come back out with the dress—it wasn't for me, whatever it was they had to do to get back right. And I didn't feel like it was for Pearl, what went on between me and Aunt Hesty in the place. I wouldn't tell her, nor nobody, what happened there. Even if I was to tell somebody exactly all the words Aunt Hesty said to me, they wouldn't be the same outside the place and her telling. I would be making a lie of it if I was to try.

While I was in my room peeling off my own wet clothes and getting into something dry, I heard Pearl come out, and after a minute her and Aunt Hesty went into the kitchen. I heard the sounds of coffee being made real loud. The clean, dry clothes felt so good on my skin. I felt I could sleep so I laid down on the bed and didn't hear another thing till the screen door slammed from Virgil and the boys coming in for supper. Supper felt normal, even though Pearl and Aunt Hesty was quiet. Neither one of them hardly spoke a word the rest of the night. While we was at the table, though, Aunt Hesty reached over and squeezed my knee, then patted it a couple of times where nobody could see. I scooted over just a tiny bit closer to her.

She said she was tired and went on to bed right after supper, so me and Pearl cleaned up by ourselves. We was about done when I went over and stood by her at the work table where she was dropping the spoons and forks into the dishpan. I stood close beside her, to where our arms was touching, elbow to shoulder.

"I'm sorry," I said.

"Well, honey," she said, "it's not for you to be sorry."

"I'm sorry it's so hard, is what I mean."

"Well, now," she said. She turned a bit and stood back from me a little then. "You look different, Linney."

"I am," I said. I felt that same kind of calm I felt after that morning I cried so much up in my clearing, all washed and dried and set right. Even though I believed everything Aunt Hesty said about things always being born and dying, right then I only felt born. I felt like I fit exactly inside my life. Right then, I was steady. The difference between the clearing and now was, this time I wasn't alone with it all.

Pearl turned so she was looking straight at me. She shifted her weight a little, then crossed her arms across her middle, each hand grabbing onto the opposite arm just above the elbow like she was holding onto herself, and she let out a breath. "Is there anything you need to tell me, Linney?" she asked.

"Oh, yes," I said. "I love you."

Aunt Hesty says that you never get used to the borning and dying. You think you do, especially when you're in the parts that feel more like borning, that you'd just as soon stay with. If you feel yourself getting used to something, she says, watch out. I understood that in my head, but the rest of me was a different story. The rest of me felt all new, like I could make anything happen.

As it was getting on toward June, seemed like the farm work settled down a little bit. There wasn't so much to figure out, Virgil said, and you could quit worrying about timing and rushing so much once you got everything in the ground. For a while it was a matter of keeping up. We didn't notice much difference in our work, Pearl and Aunt Hesty and me, but Virgil and the boys didn't always have to go right back out to work after supper. They'd go on out to the porch when they got done eating and we'd follow once we got everything all washed up and swept. Sometimes they'd be out in the yard playing horseshoes or playing cards on a little rickety table they kept out on the porch even though Pearl said it made the whole porch look broke-down and sorry. Sometimes they were talking, sometimes it got kind of rough if something had gone wrong with the day's work.

I wasn't used to boys—how they could yell and poke their fingers on each other's chests, get mad at each other right out loud. One time Danny pushed Walt backwards off the porch doing that, it was something about rocks that was supposed to be cleared out of the field and a sharp one nicked the plow blade and slowed down the whole day's work. Generally, Virgil'd put a stop to such before it got to the shoving stage, but that time it got away from him. Two shakes, though, and they was both of them out in that field digging up rocks till it was too dark to see.

Mostly it stayed quiet enough, though. Nothing like with Betts at our house. Mostly everybody was somewhere off in their heads with something in their hands they was carving or fixing. It left me feeling a little bit at loose ends, how they all kept busy with their hands. Like I didn't know where to set my eyes.

One evening, Pearl and Aunt Hesty was sitting on the porch swing piecing a quilt. They didn't know what kind yet, they said, they were just stitching up little four-patches out of a bushel basket of squares they had already cut out of feedsack scraps and old shirts and dresses and aprons. When they had a big enough pile, then they'd decide how to mix them up and put them together. I watched them and I wanted to get in there with them, but I seen how they used all their fingers for it—holding the two patches together in their left hands and wiggling the patches and the needle both back and forth to get them straight lines and tiny stitches.

"Linney, set us up some patches," Pearl said. "In pairs first, then when we get a little stack of pairs, you can set us some pairs together."

"Lord, yes," Aunt Hesty said. "It takes me longer to decide what to put together than it does for me to stitch them up." I went over and looked at the squares.

"Now, what you want," she said, "is a couple of patches that has a little something alike, maybe they both got a little bit of green in them, but otherwise is as different as you can get. Like maybe one is a plaid with a line of green in it and the other is a calico with pink posies and green leaves. They need to be friends a little bit, but if they're too much the same they're going to disappear into each other on your quilt and you won't really see neither of them. And you want

one lighter and one darker. If you can't get one lighter
and one darker, then try for one that's blue or green
and one that's red or orange or yellow."

"Good lord, Mommy, no wonder it takes you
so long. Linney, don't think about it too much, just
please your eye," Pearl said.

"I am telling her how to please the eye, Pearl."

"Well, good."

"Fine."

"Can I dump the basket?" I asked.

"Sure, honey," Pearl said.

"You'll have to be careful putting them back,"
Aunt Hesty said "so they're laying mostly flat. You
get a big wrinkled up mess, you can't hardly tell what
you're doing."

I slid my good hand in a couple inches under the
top, lifted out a layer of patches with my bad hand
on top and nudged them around on the floorboards
of the porch till I could see most of them. I sat down
cross-legged on the floor in front of the porch swing,
bending over the pile, studying on them a minute
before I picked any of them up. There was way more
plaids and solids than calicos—all them boy shirts.

"How come you didn't cut the solids into squares,
just strips?" I asked.

"We might want to sash around the four-patches
with them," Aunt Hesty said. "All them boy shirts,
they're so busy sometimes we got to settle them
down a little." She winked at me and jerked her head
over to where the boys was playing cards. "Ain't that
right, Danny?"

"You leave my shirts alone, Mamaw," he said,
but he was grinning. "I ain't the one needs settling
down."

"Really?" Doug said. "How come you need your shirt ironed before we go to town? How come that Delsie Marcus always shows up at the store when you do? How come it took you so long to get back from the barn last—" There come some quick kicking and scrabbling under the table, but Virgil cleared his throat kind of loud and Danny and Doug both took to concentrating real hard on the cards in their hands.

"Well," Pearl said. She looked over to Virgil, who give her the tiniest shrug and smile, you wouldn't have seen it if you wasn't watching for it. Kind of surprised me, that Virgil would know something Pearl didn't know. I still had my moments of seeing clear through things, like the doe.

"Hand me up some patches, Linney," Aunt Hesty said. "Maybe we better get moving if somebody's going to be needing a new quilt." Danny turned even redder, but she didn't tease him no more. Pearl was quiet too, and we all kept on with whatever we was doing till it got too dark to see what we had in our hands.

A week or so later we was out on the porch after supper like always, and here come Mr. Marcus up the road on his horse. Virgil and the boys walked down to meet him and once they got his horse settled, they all come back up to the porch.

"Al's got a fence down," Virgil told Pearl. "That big dead poplar finally give way and knocked down a whole stretch, fifty, sixty feet. They're keeping the cows and horses in the barnyard, but that's no good for long. Looks like we're going visiting."

"I promise we won't try to get you to cut fence post or dig holes," Mr. Marcus said to Pearl and Aunt

Hesty, "but Kate and the girls are sure hoping you'll come and make a day of it, stay the night if you want. The girls are real excited to meet Linney." He smiled at me, a nice smile. "Delsie's seventeen, how old are you, Linney?" I told him sixteen. "See?" he said. "You got to come."

Him and Virgil and Pearl figured it all out, that we'd go Saturday morning and come back before dark Sunday. All the time they were talking, Danny was off to the side where he'd be close enough to hear, but not hardly moving, like he didn't want to get noticed. Every once in a while, I seen him look over to where me and Aunt Hesty was sitting on the porch swing, then look away real quick. She caught him looking once.

"Now, I know things," she said, like she was talking to me, but loud. "I surely do." She waved the little pair of patches she'd just sewed together just a little bit, catching Danny's eye, before she raised it up to her mouth and bit off the thread.

Virgil was standing with his back to us. He put his hand behind his back and wagged it around at Aunt Hesty to be quiet. I figured Mr. Marcus knew enough about Aunt Hesty that he probably wasn't even listening, but Danny, he looked like he was staring down the barrel of a shotgun.

"Some people," she said, loud again, but still like she was only talking to me "feel the need to tell everything they know."

"Don't," I whispered, and elbowed her. "Look at him."

"Oh, I won't," she said out the side of her mouth. "Little scare won't hurt him none, help him take it serious, whatever it is going on."

"Now, I never was like that," she said. "That's what I like about Kate, not the kind to carry tales. I'll be so glad to see her and the girls. You're going to like them, Linney."

Mr. Marcus didn't stay long. Once he was out of earshot, Danny stomped over and stood in front of Aunt Hesty with his hands on his hips, red-faced and mad enough to spit.

"Mamaw," he said. You could see him fighting with hisself over what he wanted to say to her. I never once heard Virgil nor any of the boys say a cross word to none of us. She took account of him while he stood there trying to come up with words. She stood, reached up, took him by the shoulders and shook him just a little.

"You know why your mama's named Pearl?" she asked him. Danny wiped down his face with both hands, then clasped his hands behind his neck, shook his head and looked over to Virgil for help.

"Don't be looking at your Daddy," she said. "I'm the one talking to you."

"No, ma'am, I don't know why Mama's named Pearl." He had a little edge to his voice.

"Because she has a price beyond rubies, that's why. You think about that." She soft smacked the side of his face with her hand. "You always been a good boy, Danny," she said. "Don't you forget it."

"No, ma'am," he said. "Sorry." He looked at me and Pearl and Aunt Hesty, all three of us, like he wasn't quite sure who to be sorry to.

The boys all wandered off after that. I went in to get ready for bed, but out of the corner of my eye I seen Virgil and Pearl and Aunt Hesty standing together on the porch, looking down the road toward the Marcus place. Virgil was leaning against the porch post, and Pearl was leaning against him. Aunt Hesty stood a little apart. I stopped at the window and watched them for just a minute.

"Pretty rough on the boy," Virgil said to Aunt Hesty. "I think he's got the fear of God running through him."

"It's well he should," said Pearl.

Aunt Hesty shook her head. Who knows what all she was thinking of in that moment—I was remembering everything she'd told me out on the rock over the creek that morning.

"Hell, yes," she said.

June 14, 1910

Dear Robbie,

It is big news here, about Danny and Delsie Marcus. We all of us went up there for a couple of days last week, for your daddy and the boys to help Mr. Marcus mend fence. I wasn't sure I really wanted to go. I was just starting to feel kind of normal, you know, like I could live here, like I do live here. It feels so different from home, Robbie. I never knew till I got here how much of me just don't show when I'm at home. Almost everything that happens to me there happens on the inside, and nobody ever asks me what I'm thinking. I'm trying to change that while I'm here, I'm trying to say things out loud.

You know when I felt like I really belonged? When your mama asked me one day was there anything I needed to tell her. It's like having a whole house to live in instead of living inside one tiny room. Anyway, I was feeling good and wanting to hold on and hold still, but we were going to Marcus's.

Maybe you already knew about Danny and

Delsie. Doug already knew and he let the cat out of the bag one night on the porch after supper, so we all of us had a pretty good idea. Aunt Hesty give Danny a hard time about it, but he took it like a man, as Daddy says. All that week before we went, I felt Danny watching me. One morning when I went out to dump the dishwater, he was waiting around the corner of the house and waving me over. I went over, but he just stood there crossing and uncrossing his arms, and shifting his weight back and forth, and looking at his feet. Finally, I had to ask him, "Danny, what do you need?" He says, "I don't know about girls, Linney. What kinds of things do girls like?"

Well, now, I have to say, I don't know what girls like either, not the way I figured he meant. I asked him what did he mean, and he said, for presents. He was wanting to take her a present. I never had a present from a boy, nor a boy I wanted a present from, so I still didn't know what to tell him. I thought a minute and then told him about my box Daddy made me, I figured that was the best present I ever got. "What do you keep in it?" he asked me. And I told him a little, but not everything. "Some of it's personal," I told him. I told him it's to hold my best things. He didn't have time to make nothing like that, but I said to tell her he was making something for her. That's what I liked so much about my box, Daddy taking all that care to make it.

"I'll show it to you after supper," I said, "so you can get an idea how you want to do hers." He was smiling by then, he couldn't help it. You should have seen him, now I know why people call it being sweet on somebody. He hugged me and whispered

"Thanks, Linney" in my ear, then let go and headed out toward the barn and the fields. He turned back after a few steps though, walking backwards, and said "Don't tell." I covered my mouth with my hand and shook my head. And I won't. I'm only telling you, which is not the same as carrying tales or teasing like Aunt Hesty.

They worked so hard and long on the fence over at Marcus's, there wasn't hardly any time except for eating that we was all together. I think Mrs. Marcus knew something, for she only set the table for the grownups and sent the rest of us out to eat on the porch. Danny and Delsie sat on the steps and the rest of us tried not to keep looking at them. And all through the day Mrs. Marcus and your mama sent me and Delsie out to carry water to them working out there on the fence. No need to hurry back, they said. Me and her was out there when they finished up. We all of us walked back in little clumps— Virgil and Tom and Mr. Marcus out in front, then Doug, Walt and me with a couple of the Beecham boys, and Danny and Delsie falling behinder and behinder. The sun was getting low and it was a good feeling to be walking back with everybody.

There's more to tell about the visit, but to get to the big news-two days after we got home, Danny went walking by himself over to Marcus's, and him and Delsie will get married in the fall. Aunt Hesty has give him a little silver ring to give her, and Mrs. Marcus has her daddy's ring for Danny to marry with. We are working every night on that quilt, and Aunt Hesty, as you probably can figure, keeps saying all kinds of things to Danny that keeps him red as a barn. But she keeps saying "good boy" too, so he's not mad—I don't think he could be mad about anything right now if he tried. I couldn't wait to write and tell you because of course you will be coming home for the wedding, and I feel happy thinking about it.

Your mama, though, is a little bit quiet, Robbie. It's looking like Danny and Delsie will live over at Marcus's. There is a little house on the place, from the people who lived there before, a little house with two rooms and a kitchen just right for somebody that's just setting up housekeeping. It's not been much took care of, but Virgil says it's got good bones and they can fix it up and add on rooms as they go along. Seems like everybody gets a little quiet when Danny talks about that place. It makes sense, Daddy would say, for Danny to go over there, since they have only got three girls and no boys. But I don't think it makes sense to your mama, not all the way. At least they are only the next farm over and not a whole county away. She says to tell you she is writing you a letter too, she's just slow at it, and to write her a letter when you can. Me, too, Robbie. I don't know if it makes sense but being happy makes me miss you more.

love, yr. sister,
Linney

Some things are harder to put down in words than they are to talk about. There was something solider about writing that made me feel like I needed to have things figured out before I wrote them down, or at least I needed to be on my way to figuring them out by writing them down. Part of what made me feel so jangled while we was getting ready to go to the Marcus's was all them sisters. Delsie might be alright if Danny was sweet on her, but then there was one named Katie, after her mama, that was fourteen like Betts, and another one they called Ollie that was just twelve. Who knew how it would be when Delsie married Danny and turned into a sister.

I kept going back to that picture in my head of Aunt Hesty on the rock, telling me that generally speaking she'd got no use for sisters. If I'd had any more room for shock in me that morning, that would have shocked me. Not that she felt that way about it, but that somebody would say such a thing right out loud. I told Betts I hated her that morning at the kitchen table, but that was different from Aunt Hesty saying it like it was just good common sense and nothing to be ashamed of.

I'm not much for church, but Mama makes us all go whenever there's a real preacher comes around. Every once in a while they come and set up a tent down by the main road. I never forgot one that preached on the camel and the eye of the needle and he said any little sin will keep you out of Heaven and send you straight to Hell. You have to be sure you repent at the end of every day for every sin, for if you forget one, even a little one that just slipped your mind, no matter what it is, that's enough to keep you from going through the eye of that needle and to send you down to Hell to burn alive forever and ever. And he said—by which I mean he screamed and pounded on the pulpit and sweated rivers and about throwed his shoulder out of its socket pointing at people—he said it had to be true repentance, that you suffered over, that made you crawl and weep, and rend your garments and tear your hair.

Mama'd made us get there real early so we was on the front bench and I could smell his stink from where we were. You couldn't help but be scared. It was on toward night and the corners of the tent was all shadowy and dark, the shadows shifting around on account of the lamps they had set up in the corners, and people standing up and praying, then sitting back down groaning. I could feel the hair lifting on my arms like it was singeing off. I figured there was no saving me—I would go to Hell for not loving my sister, and because I couldn't be sorry. So when Mr. Marcus come around talking about his girls, well, I just didn't care to be reminded about all that sister mess. I'd just as soon stay out of it.

When we got to the Marcus place that morning, Mrs. Marcus and the girls was out on the porch. Mrs. Marcus said Mr. Marcus had gone out to the fence at first daylight with a couple of the Beecham boys who'd come over to help. The poplar hadn't just knocked the fenceposts over, it had knocked them into splinters, she said, so it was going to be a pile of work to cut all them new fenceposts and get them set in. Virgil and the boys settled the horses while me and Pearl and Aunt Hesty carried up from the wagon the stack cake and dried apple pies we made yesterday to bring with us. Mrs. Marcus had a big pot of coffee on the stove and a plate of biscuits with a crock of molasses butter. Their back porch faced west, so it wasn't too warm already to sit out there with that good coffee and them biscuits. Mrs. Marcus and Pearl took up on the porch swing, Aunt Hesty took the rocker, and the two littler Marcus girls seemed to have their own places sitting on the steps. I stood there a minute with my plate and cup of coffee, wanting to stick with Pearl and Aunt Hesty, but not knowing where to put myself.

Delsie was sitting on the porch floor, leaning her back against the porch rails with her legs straight out and crossed at the ankles, facing the porch swing and rockers. She didn't say nothing, just patted the place beside her and I sat down there. That was nice. We weren't little girls to be sitting on the steps, we were with the women.

"Linney, we just been waiting and waiting to meet you," Mrs. Marcus said. "All of us, but Delsie especially. It's a good thing when you're young to have somebody your own age around. You remember them days, Pearl, when it was me and you?"

"I surely do," Pearl said, and she leaned her head for a minute over onto Mrs. Marcus's shoulder. "I'd have never got out of the house if it wasn't for you. Mommy watched on me so hard, I liked to never got out from under her big eye, but she'd let me come stay at your house every once in a while. That's how I met Virgil, Linney, his daddy knew Kate's daddy and they'd come visiting over to Kate's sometimes when I was there."

"Every time, you mean," Mrs. Marcus said.

They both of them looked at me and Delsie sitting there beside each other on the floor with our plates and smiled at each other some kind of smile that only they knew what it meant.

"Lord," Mrs. Marcus said.

"—help us," Pearl added.

I looked over at Delsie and her face was red as fire. It wasn't like we all didn't know about her and Danny, but nobody was saying it out loud. Aunt Hesty'd been awful quiet. She'd huffed a little bit when Pearl talked about meeting Virgil at Mrs. Marcus's house, but now she was looking at us too. She stared at us with them eyes till we both had to look away. She shifted around in the rocker and harrumphed a little. Her voice was rough.

"Beautiful," she said.

Me and Delsie looked at each other then, so surprised to hear that, so surprised to see in each other's faces that it was so. I thought she must have already known, how could she not? She was pretty everywhere, curly everywhere, even around her eyes and mouth. Her hair was darkish red, she had brown eyes and little light freckles on her nose and cheeks. In her body she was strong looking and round all at the same time. Me, on the other hand, I never thought of myself as even pretty, just ordinary, nothing bad wrong with me except for my hand.

But when Aunt Hesty said that, whatever I was become beautiful. I felt that knowing come on me, like after our time in the place. It was like she named us, me and Delsie together, give us that word, beautiful, like a name from another place, that showed us truer and deeper than our given names ever could. It made us, I don't know, twins almost, even though we hadn't yet even spoken a word to each other.

Mrs. Marcus and Pearl were still staring at us.

"Virgil and Al and them's going to be needing some water and something to eat out there," Aunt Hesty said, how she does, out of the blue sometimes like you're not already in the middle of something else. "You all go on now," she said, flapping her hand at me and Delsie. "Take the little ones with you and carry them out what they need."

Mrs. Marcus and Pearl shook themselves out of staring at us and got up and put together a basket of ham biscuits and sausage biscuits and give that to Katie to carry. They handed Ollie a basket of coffee cups. I took a pot of coffee from Mrs. Marcus and Delsie picked up a clean bucket to fill up at the pump on the way.

"You all get on, now," Aunt Hesty said, shooing us again.

We headed out, we was at the edge of the yard and I heard Mrs. Marcus say, "Look at them go."

"Don't I know it," Pearl said.

When we turned the corner around the barn and was out of sight and out of hearing, Delsie stopped in her tracks and looked at me. Katie and Ollie stopped too, but she told them to go on, we'd be right there. Katie made a face at Delsie, but she went on.

"Well," Delsie said. She set down the bucket and stood there looking at me with her arms hanging down by her sides, but with her palms turned out like a question.

"I know," I said.

"It's like—" but she couldn't think of what it was like. It wasn't like anything else.

"We don't have to figure it out," I told her. "It's enough just to know it."

We walked slower the rest of the way to the fence line. We carried ourselves like women, like women who didn't hurry for nobody. We didn't say much, we didn't need to. When we got in sight of where they was working, Virgil called out, "Now, who are them beautiful ladies bringing us coffee?"

Delsie looked at me. "They don't know the half of it, do they?" she said.

"Not yet," I said, "but I expect they will."

When we got back, Mrs. Marcus and Pearl and Aunt Hesty was full into making dinner. Mrs. Marcus was slicing a ham to fry up, Pearl was cutting up a chicken and Aunt Hesty was peeling potatoes. They put the little girls to helping with the potatoes and Mrs. Marcus sent me and Delsie out on the porch with a big mess of green beans to string and break. We sat on the porch swing with the basket of beans between us, a big piece of brown paper on the floor for the strings and ends, and the kettle on the other side of that.

"I don't think I can do it," I told Delsie. She'd already done a whole handful and was dropping the pieces into the kettle. They made a tinny little raining noise as they fell in.

"How about if I string a little pile and you break them, want to try that?" Mama had tried that with me before, but I'd been so slow she got all aggravated and said it'd be quicker to just do it herself.

"I'm pretty fast," Delsie said. "It'll all balance out, it won't matter if you're a little slow."

We got going, how she said, and I wasn't as slow as I thought I'd be. I picked up a little speed as we went along. She started talking about the Chandlers.

"We been around them long as I can remember, Aunt Pearl and Mama's been best friends since they was girls, well, you already know that. I always had it in my head the three of us girls would marry three of the Chandler boys and since I was oldest, I figured it would be Tom. When I was a little girl, I mean, I figured it would be Tom. But a year or so ago, it was Danny trying to sit by me when they come over and telling me things and laughing so much. Once last summer we was over there and Aunt Pearl sent us out for a little more corn for supper. When we was walking out there he just kind of stopped and looked at me. It took him a minute, but then he said he figured I knew if I ever needed anything, I should tell him. I said, 'I expect I do know that,' and from then on it was him and me."

She talked on, and then I told about Robbie and Mama and Betts. "Ugh," she'd say every once in a while while I was telling it all and make a little shuddery shake with her shoulders. Or "Ouch," she'd say. "Oh, Linney."

When I told her about the penny and what all I'd been figuring out about deciding who I would be, her fingers stopped working the beans and she looked full at me.

"Yes," she said. She looked off toward where the boys was working and said it again, "Yes."

Then the beans were done, and we had to go in and see what else needed done in the kitchen. Virgil and Al and all the boys came and went from dinner. The grownups ate inside, and we all ate out on the porch, Danny and Delsie down on the steps and the rest of us sitting around in little bunches. I had Walt beside me on the porch swing and both the Beecham boys sitting across, where me and Delsie had sat that morning on the porch floor. By the time we got everything cleaned up after dinner, it was almost time to be thinking about supper. We come out on the porch to breathe a minute, it was steaming hot in the kitchen.

Aunt Hesty was looking pretty used up, so Pearl sent her to one of the back bedrooms to rest with a rag and a basin of cool water. Pearl and Mrs. Marcus went back to the porch swing with cool rags too and started fanning their faces with their aprons.

"Let's go cool off at the pump," Delsie said to me, and we both of us looked over to the porch swing.

"Go ahead on," Pearl said. "No boys around, might as well get it while you can."

Delsie pumped and when the water splashed out, I couldn't believe how much I craved to be in it. I put my head underneath and run my fingers up through my hair till it was soaked through. I unbuttoned my dress a little and let the cold water run down my front, my back, then hiked up my skirt and let it run down my legs. My whole body had got so thirsty. Then Delsie had a turn, and we seen Katie and Ollie running toward us. They'd come out on the porch and found out what we was doing, so we pumped for them too and took another turn ourselves, for that was how hot it was. One of their dogs come out of the shade from the barn, a middling-sized brown dog with rough looking fur, skinny legs and stand-up ears. He come sniffing around at the cold-water smell and we splashed the water onto his back and legs then held the water, so fresh and cold, cupped in our hands and let him drink as long as he wanted. I could feel my hair already getting dry from the sun. I looked at Delsie standing there dripping in the sun.

"Do you still feel it?" I asked her, though I could see plain as day she did. She just raised both her arms up toward the sun, and her face was shiny with water.

"What, feel what?" Katie asked. We couldn't say it—beautiful—she didn't have ears for it yet. It was our turn for it.

"Never mind," Delsie said to her, and Katie rolled her eyes and groaned.

When we got back to the porch, she was still mad. "Delsie and Linney are keeping secrets," she told her mother before she even got all the way up the steps. I felt my steps and my breath too slow down just a little bit.

"That's what secrets are for," Mrs. Marcus said. "Everybody's got a right to their own things, Katie, you know that."

Katie stomped around for a while but nobody paid it any mind and it was over by suppertime. "How simple was that?" I thought but I kept it to myself.

The men had got the fence work all done except for three or four posts Mr. Marcus said he could manage hisself, so nobody had to go back out to work. Pearl and Mrs. Marcus had done up enough biscuits and cornbread at dinnertime to where they didn't have to bake again for supper. We had big plates of sliced tomatoes and cukes, and the rest of the chicken and ham, and the stack cake and pies we brought with us. We all of us ate out on the porch, it was too hot in the house. There was little spatters of talk, but everybody was tired. One of the Beecham boys had brought his guitar and he got it out and played a little bit. The tunes was pretty, but I didn't like the words, songs about girls drowned in rivers and such as that. When Virgil started to snore in one of the rockers, Mrs. Marcus got up and called it bedtime. We'd brought quilts and pillows with us for pallets. The grownups took the beds, all us girls slept in pallets in the front room, and the boys out on the porch. I wisht we was out on the porch, for the cool, but we kept the windows open and it was alright. Delsie made up her pallet under the front window, and when I fell asleep I was hearing her and Danny talking, not really the words, just the shapes of their talk.

I didn't want to go to sleep, I didn't want it to be over. Then it was morning, and time to go.

Aunt Hesty had been awful quiet during most of the visit. I had to be glad about that, it give me time to be with Delsie. I was wanting to sit by Aunt Hesty in the wagon on the way home, though. It wasn't I had anything much to say, I just wanted to feel her there. But when we was getting into the wagon to come home, Virgil said to pile in close and we'd give the Beecham boys a ride back to their place. They'd all worked so hard, he said, he didn't want to send anybody out walking. I got jostled apart from Aunt Hesty and ended up at the back end of the wagon next to Ted Beecham, the one with the guitar. He was a nice-looking boy, but something about him felt real different from the Chandler boys.

I never been the kind of girl that boys pay attention to. I maybe tried a couple of times at church to talk to one of them, just to see, but I felt so dumb while I was doing it that I just quit. I didn't even like to think about it most of the time. And now here was this Ted Beecham, asking me did I have a favorite song, and he would learn it if I did. I knew what was happening from seeing it happen to other girls—the boys trying to get the girls to look, instead of the other way around. I tried to think if I had a favorite song. I thought of Aunt Hesty in the kitchen doing her version of "Jesus Loves Me," and I just couldn't think of no other songs after that.

"I don't know," I said. "My daddy don't play, so I don't know many songs except for church songs and I don't like any of them all that much."

"Maybe I can think of some you'd like," Ted said. "Maybe next time you're at Delsie's I'll come down and play some for you."

"That'd be nice," I said. He looked the other way and smiled, but I seen it. We was to the Beecham place by then. "Bye, Linney," he said, "Tell Danny to tell Delsie to tell me next time you're coming." Both boys jumped out of the wagon and stood there waving till we turned out of sight.

I got back with Aunt Hesty and rode the rest of the way home resting myself against her.

It should have been a lot more fun, I was thinking, to have a boy wanting to sing me songs. By the time we got home, I'd figured it out some. All day I knew I was beautiful—that was what made him look. And it was that same thing that made it not matter all that much whether he did or not.

It started turning into a rainy summer after we come back from Marcus's. On the one hand, this was good because everything was growing. On the other hand, it was a lot more work because everything was growing—not just what you'd planted, but every kind of weed and snaky vine you could name, plus a few you'd swear you'd never seen before. Me and Pearl and Aunt Hesty, we couldn't hardly keep up with hoeing and pulling weeds out in the kitchen garden. Pearl begun counting jars and thinking about whether to spend money on more, there was so many tomatoes and cukes and green beans coming on. We maybe ought to can some green tomatoes, she was saying, for there was a limit to how much canning could get done between the time the tomatoes would be ready and the time they'd begin to get soft and rot. We was just coming into full summer and already she was thinking about what could be saved.

One morning we woke up to a light gray drizzling rain, but the sky got darker and the rain steadier as we got breakfast on the table and we figured we'd not see the sun that day. It was washing day too. Some of the boys' clothes looked more like they was made out of mud than out of cloth.

"What if we just pinned everything up on the clothesline," I said to Pearl, I was cracking eggs and looking out the window up at the sky, "and let the rain have at it? If it does anything like it did last week, I bet most of the mud would be gone by the end of the day."

"Well, if we knew we'd have sun tomorrow it might be worth a try," said Pearl. "But we might just end up with a pile of wet clothes getting all musty smelling in the house to go along with the damp we already got."

Virgil and Tom come into the kitchen just then. They got their coffee and sat down, planning what all kinds of work they could do in the barn for the day—seeing if any of the wagon wheels needed fixed or replaced, sharpening up the hoes, such as that. "Nothing to stop us from dragging in some loose wood out of the thicket," Virgil said, "and cutting some fencepost—we don't want to get caught out, anything happens over here like over at the Marcus place." The other boys come in, grumbling but quiet when they heard what Virgil and Tom had in mind for them. It could get a body to feeling hemmed in, a string of rainy days like that. It got me to wondering what the Tug looked like these days, it was always so pretty when it was full. I wondered if Robbie would be down there with his pole right then, what he would be thinking about the wedding and all. We was still waiting for a letter back from him.

When the boys had gone out to the barn and left us to ourselves, we sat at the table with coffee for a bit and talked about Danny and Delsie. Pearl was thinking we'd have enough out of the kitchen garden to set them up with a nice supply of canned goods for part of their wedding present, if she could talk Virgil into getting some more jars.

"Pearl Chandler," Aunt Hesty said, "you ain't never had to talk Virgil into nor out of anything. You just tell him and it's done."

"Now that's for true," Pearl said. "Don't I know it."

What about Robbie? I thought, but I didn't say.

The more I felt like I belonged there with them, the more that question started to matter to me. I couldn't figure out why Pearl had let it happen. But I couldn't think about it too much. It scared me to think too far about what might make Pearl let somebody go.

"You and Delsie," Aunt Hesty said to me, like it was a question.

I smiled, I couldn't help it. I felt more awake ever since we got back from the Marcus place. Everything felt lighter and clearer knowing there was somebody like me, that saw things like I did, right up the road.

Aunt Hesty was staring at me, them eyebrows drawing in, while Pearl got up and got the coffee pot and emptied it out between our three cups. "I don't know," Aunt Hesty said.

"About what?" Pearl asked.

"Sisters."

"Delsie's just Delsie, Mommy," Pearl said. "Nobody else."

Aunt Hesty took to tapping her spoon on the table, the way she'd tapped that knitting needle up in the cave. She looked back and forth between me and Pearl, there was something she wasn't saying. We waited for her to say it, whatever it was, but she just kept tapping. Finally, Pearl reached across the table and laid her hand over Aunt Hesty's.

"Anyway," she said, "I got a feeling Linney's no fool when it comes to sisters, are you Linney?" I covered my mouth with my hand, I don't know why, and shook my head no.

"You got any bad feeling about Delsie?" Pearl went on, still looking at me and holding Aunt Hesty's hand with the spoon down on the table, "Are you worried about having her for a sister, Linney?"

I put my hand down off my mouth. "No," I said. "I want her. I don't care if she's my sister or cousin or whatever."

"See there, Mommy," Pearl said. "Linney's not worried, why are you?"

Aunt Hesty snatched her hand out from under Pearl's and threw the spoon across the room. She stood up, one hand on the table to steady herself on the table and wagged her finger at Pearl with the other. "She'll be the death of us—" the words came out so loud and fast that Pearl jumped back and I did too, I almost fell off my chair. Aunt Hesty pounded the table and almost lost her balance herself.

"You know it," she said, "Linney does too."

She was pointing at me, her whole arm shaking as Pearl rounded the corner of the table to make sure she didn't fall.

"I'll not have the two of you sitting there talking to me all calm like you all know everything there is to know in this world about everything. You don't know what can happen—" Her voice was going up and up and Pearl was trying to hug her quiet. She got her back into her chair and stood behind her, hugging Aunt Hesty around her chest from behind. Pearl looked at me then, and I nodded, I knew what Aunt Hesty was talking about.

"Well, now," she said to Aunt Hesty, her chin on top of her mama's head. Aunt Hesty was twitching her arms around like she was going to break Pearl's hold on her, and she was glaring at me. "You've taught her good, then. She'll know trouble if she sees it."

Aunt Hesty looked at me. I knew what it was. She was scared for me. She loved me.

"I can smell it a mile away," I said, to her and Pearl both.

"Good girl," they both of them said at once.

Good for me, was what they meant. Not what Mama and Daddy meant when they said it, which was good for everybody else's sake, good at keeping the peace.

I picked up our coffee cups and carried them over to the dishpan under the window. I looked out and seen Virgil hurrying to the house, Aunt Hesty must have been hollering loud enough for him to hear out at the barn. I caught his eye and shook my head and waved him back. He stood there in the rain a minute, not sure, then raised one hand back to me and run back to the barn. By the time I turned around, Pearl and Aunt Hesty had pulled themselves apart. Pearl was on all fours, fishing that spoon out from under the worktable and Aunt Hesty was through the house somewhere. I heard the screen door slam. Pearl stood and straightened up with the spoon in one hand, and pushed back her hair then smoothed down her apron front with the other.

"Good thing I still had my apron on," she said, pointing to coffee spatter all down her front. She looked up at me. "It's good she told you, Linney. It's good you know."

I stared at Pearl. It was too much to get my head around, whatever it was that just happened.

"Best run after her," she said. "Won't do for her to be getting out of sight when she's like that."

Good. Good girl. For once I was hearing them words without feeling like somebody was trying to take me for a fool. Good to know when things were wrong. Good to know the whole story, no matter what it was. That was good, finally.

Dog Days

AUGUST 1910

IT JUST KEPT GETTING HOTTER and hotter. By the beginning of August, we woke up hot, there wasn't no part of the day you could count on for a little cool. Me and Pearl and Aunt Hesty would make up breakfast quick as we could and we all carried our plates out to the porch to eat, to spare ourselves the heat from the stove and the close quarters in the kitchen. Almost every afternoon around two it rained, a straight down rain like somebody emptying out a bucket. It'd be over inside of an hour and then steam the rest of the afternoon. You could see it coming up off the roof of the barn and low places in the fields. Virgil started saying pretty soon we'd not even need the kitchen—everything was getting cooked before it was even picked.

Pearl started talking about canning before the green beans and tomatoes started to rot on the vine from too much rain—but it was hard to imagine whole days in the kitchen with the stove full on, washing and boiling jars, filling them up with steaming tomatoes and beans, then setting the jars back in the boiling water bath till they finished and sealed—batch after batch, bushel after bushel. And that was just tomatoes and beans. It would all have to be done, but we was holding off, hoping for a break in the heat.

"No wonder they call it dog days," Doug said one day when they was all back to the house for dinner. Me and Pearl had tacked up a sheet to hang down from the porch roof on one end, to make a little more shade. We'd cooked up some greens with vinegar and set out tomato and onion slices. Pearl did the cornbread right after breakfast then put it down in the root cellar to get cool. We broke it up in bowls and poured cold milk over it. Even so, nobody felt much like eating.

"I feel like a old dog, how they find some shade and just lay there and can't do nothing but pant," Doug went on. "Remember back in February when we had to start figuring out how much stove wood we could use every day, to make it last till spring? How cold it got in the house? Sounds kind of good, don't it?"

"Maybe we can go down to the creek before we go back," Walt said. "Keep our clothes on, wet clothes help a little." They were out in the corn, pulling off viney weeds that were growing up the stalks. They couldn't roll up their sleeves or pant legs while they worked, those corn leaves are sharp as blades, you'd come out all sliced up in tiny cuts.

"Now, that's not right," Aunt Hesty said, looking at Doug. "It's a story, dog days, is what it is. An old story. My daddy told it to me, he was a judge you know, he'd been to school, he knew some things. Most of it dull as dirt, but some of it was stories."

Nobody wanted to hurry off the porch. Even Virgil leaned back in his chair. "Tell it, Mommy," Pearl said.

Aunt Hesty set her plate on the floor beside the rocker, picked up her glass of water and held it in her hand at the end of the arm of the rocker. She leaned her head back, begun to rock just a little and to talk up into the air.

"Way back when, across the ocean, across the sea, before any of them over there in Greece even knowed there was such a place as Kentucky, there was a powerful hunter, name of Orion. When he was still a boy he was the best hunter in the county, best hunter in the state, then by the time he was a grown man he was the best hunter in the whole country and in the whole world.

Now, he was a braggy one. Or maybe not, you know how people find ways to talk somebody down that's really good at something, so I don't know. But he was always bringing home the biggest boar, that's a wild pig, and the biggest stag, that's a deer, and the most of whatever it was everybody was out hunting. Pretty soon, people started getting jealous and talking about did he have some kind of secret, some kind of deal with the Devil or one of the gods. Come to think of it, though, I don't think they had the Devil back then, I think the devil-type business just got parceled out between all the gods, they all had part devil in them. Which sounds about right to me, I have to say.

Anyway, the other thing about them gods was, some of them was women and the woman gods did things like hunting and making war and all kinds of trouble out in the world, just like the men. There was a woman god named Artemis and she was a hunter too. She was famous for what she could do with a bow and arrow. She wasn't jealous of Orion though, she loved him with all her heart even though she was a woman god and he was just a human man.

Well, now, them gods, sometimes they was a wee bit childish, by which I mean, a lot. This god Apollo, he was the sun god so he figured he was kind of a big deal and Artemis ought to love him instead. So what he did was, he got Artemis looking at a tiny little speck bobbing out in the sea and he double-dog-dared her to try and shoot it with an arrow. I expect she didn't mind showing him what for, so that's what she did."

"I don't see what this has got to do with dog days, Mamaw," Walt said. "Daddy's not going to let us go to the creek if we sit here much longer."

Aunt Hesty took a long slow drink from her glass, then kept on like she'd not heard him. "What she didn't know, now, till Apollo told her, was that little speck was Orion, and she'd just killed him dead with her bow and arrow. I reckon it was pretty hot that day," she leaned over in Walt's direction and raised that one eyebrow at him, "and he was wanting to cool off before he went back out to the hunt."

Danny give Walt a push on his shoulder, then drew back his arm like he was aiming a bow and arrow. "It's a good story, Mamaw," Doug said, "but I don't see what it's got to do with dog days neither."

"You ever know a hunter not to have a dog?" Aunt Hesty asked, talking up into the air again. "Well, wouldn't a powerful hunter have a powerful lot of powerful good hunting dogs? And there's always one, isn't there, that has the best nose, and runs the fastest, and loves him best. That was Serious. Every day Serious went down to the shore of the sea and cried and howled and run up and down looking for Orion. Lord, that is an awful thing to see, we've seen it plenty, ain't we, Pearl, man dies and leaves a dog behind."

Serious wasn't never going to find Orion, not even his washed-up body there, for Artemis was so sorry and grief-struck when she found out what she'd done, that she turned Orion into stars and put him up in the sky where she could see him all the time. You can see him at night, like you can see the big dipper if you know what you're looking for. So, what Artemis did was, she put Serious up there with him, bright bluish looking star right at his heel. Dog star, people call it."

"I wonder if he was a blue tick," Doug said.

"I don't know about them Greek dogs," Aunt Hesty said. "But when you see Orion and Serious up there by the sun when it's coming up, that's when it's getting to be dog days. You can see Orion's got the string of his bow pulled back, and the curve of it, and his sword hanging down off his belt. And Serious right there by his side. They're chasing that sun god, fixing to run him out of the county, is what I always think.

Way back when, Daddy used to say, they'd watch for the dog star to show up over there in Egypt, and that'd tell them to get ready for the Nile to flood." She leaned back over toward Walt again, reached out and give him a big pinch on the arm. "So they could cool off, I reckon."

Walt pulled his arm away, but him and Doug were both looking up at the sky. "I wish it was dark now," Doug said. "I wish we could see them."

Virgil stood up with his plate and glass in his hand. "You all carry your dishes in," he said. "Go get a good soaking at the creek but come back before it clouds up."

Aunt Hesty followed Doug and Walt in through the front door and poking them in the back with her finger. "Watch out for arrows," she said, making little hissing sounds like flying arrows to go with every poke.

Later on when I was helping wash up after supper, I was thinking how nice it was to sit out on the porch and hear a story. It struck me I was going days on end without thinking about home. If it wasn't for thinking about Robbie, maybe I wouldn't be wanting to think about it at all.

But there was something sticking in my craw I couldn't get all the way shed of. The thing was, Pearl had begun to talk about Robbie coming home for the wedding, but nobody ever said anything about afterwards. There would still be some weeks of work bringing in the crops, and I didn't know what all had to be done with the tobacco Daddy was growing, but I knew there was a lot to it. So I knew Robbie would go back again after the wedding, but for how long?

And whenever that question come up in me, which was happening more and more, it brought another question right with it that about stopped me in my tracks. What would they do about me when it was time for him to come back for good?

The day Virgil and Pearl come for me, I wisht I'd had time to get strong about my plan to decide who I would be. Nothing waits till you're ready. Maybe that's good, maybe you never are ready for the big things. Turned out that it was after I got here, with Pearl and Aunt Hesty and all of them, that I got strong. I had that picture in my head of asking Pearl in the kitchen what to call her, and Aunt Hesty telling me her whole story out on the rock. There was Virgil asking me did I need anything, and Walt saying "Ladies first." Danny asking me about girls. Delsey and me knowing we was beautiful.

I didn't have to get strong to hold my own against them like I thought in the beginning. It was them held me, like I was their own.

"You're awful quiet today," Pearl said. We was almost done cleaning up, and I'd been standing at the worktable looking out the window and twisting a dish rag since that thought about Robbie and going home had caught me off guard. "You feeling alright, Linney?"

"Yes," I said. "I don't know."

"What don't you know, honey?" she asked.

I turned and looked at her. I was not of a mind yet to ask any questions I didn't want to hear the answers to. I turned back around and tried to think what might really help me. Tomorrow was Sunday, I almost always got some time off to myself on Sundays.

"I might like to go see Delsie," I said. "Do you think they'd mind if I just showed up tomorrow? I can walk, we've gone enough now, I know the way."

"One of the boys'll walk you over," Pearl said.

I looked at Pearl and Aunt Hesty both. "I need to walk," I said. Those were Aunt Hesty's words for when she'd decide out of the blue she felt like taking off.

"I don't like it," Pearl said, but Aunt Hesty said I could take along little pieces of the blue and green they were thinking about using for the back of Danny's and Delsie's quilt and find out which one she liked the best, without giving away what it was for, of course.

"It'll take you about an hour and a half walking, so you can start out right after breakfast," Pearl said, after she spent a minute or two wiping at a spot of grease on the table. "But you be back here by suppertime, so I don't even have to think about worrying about you."

I promised. After supper I said I was tired and wanted to lay down for a little while. When I got in my room, I got my box from Daddy out from under my bed and sat there on the edge of the bed looking at it in my lap. I traced the name he'd carved on it with my finger, Caroline. Who had Mama and Daddy imagined, that would fit that name? And why had Daddy put it on my box instead of Linney, the name I'd turned out to be? I put the box back under my bed without opening it up and laid back on the bed and closed my eyes.

I knew that penny was in there, but I didn't know what was mine to decide.

I felt like I was holding my breath, waiting to get to Delsie. I had a terrible need to say everything out loud all at once to somebody that could hear it all, and it couldn't be Pearl or Aunt Hesty or even Robbie this time. They were all too mixed up in it with me, in all my questions about going back home. My head felt crammed full and hollow all at the same time. I put my hands on my face to try and quiet my head, then covered my eyes, and next thing I knew it was morning.

It's a longish walk to Marcus's, but not hard. There's a path runs straight behind the fields along the edge of the woods here for a ways, and then it goes crooked and cuts through the woods till you come back out to a straight path again behind the fields at the Marcus place. Most of the path is through the woods, but it's easy to see and there's only one stretch that's hilly. Pearl made me up a little sack with some cornbread wrapped up in a towel and a quart jar of water and a handkerchief in case I needed to tie up my hair, for it was plenty hot already. It was a little sack with shoulder straps I could wear on my back, the boys said it kept you from feeling loaded down. The little fabric scraps for the quilt she tucked into my pocket.

"Be sure you fill up the water jar before you start back," Virgil said. They was all standing out on the back porch after breakfast, watching me go, like they could tell something was happening but they didn't know what it was. I was in a hurry and I couldn't pretend like I wasn't. Seemed like it left them feeling unsettled, how I wanted to go off, all for except Danny who had grumped his way all through breakfast that anybody but him would be going off to see Delsie. So I was glad when I got to where the path turned off into the woods. I turned and looked back to wave. Virgil and Pearl and Aunt Hesty was standing there the way they were that night after Mr. Marcus had come to ask for help with their fence. They waved back and stayed there watching as I went on into the woods. I wondered what they were saying to each other, but not for long. It was what I was going to say that mattered, and I wouldn't know what it was till I heard myself say it.

It felt like the heat eased off some when I got under the trees, though it didn't take long for that feeling to wear off. I'd walked fast from the house to the woods, and I couldn't slow my steps down right away. I was keeping ahead of those questions that was catching up with me. But the woods slowed me down. There's places won't be hurried through.

I didn't know I'd been missing my little clearing up the hill at home till I got a ways into the woods and begun to feel alone in there. It was the good kind of alone, the kind that fits you exactly. There's nothing around you that's not real, so you feel more real too, more like yourself. I got quieter in my head. My steps calmed down, and I started looking around. The shine was mostly off the tree-top leaves, like it always was by August, but there'd been so much rain it had got through the leaves, down to the ground. The underbrush was thick with viney plants in full leaf going up the tree trunks and tiny-leafed mossy plants spreading out into the path. Forget the stars in the sky or the sands in the desert, like they talk about in the Bible, I thought. Try counting the leaves in the woods.

I walked a long while, laying eyes on the leaves, letting my eyes do my thinking for me. All my questions about who would have me and what I really wanted were alive and lit up inside me. For the moment, it seemed like enough to carry the questions through all the spreading, shifting leaves.

I was getting ready for something. There was no words to it, it was calm, almost restful.

The air smelled like wet wood and warm weeds, on the edge of rank in some spots I passed through. I started having to watch my step when I got to the low-lying stretch, for the rain had puddled up across the path. Where it sat puddled on the ground for a long time it got slick and muddied deeper than you'd think. I walked two or three feet into the brush to get around the bigger puddles, till I took a fall on some slick leaves and messed up the back of my dress. Then I started jumping the smaller ones if I figured I could. I begun to feel in a hurry again, like somebody that's lost, and thinking I should have been out of the woods by then, wondering if I'd took a wrong turn even though I could see the path. I was getting a pretty bad feeling till I come on a jog in the path, right before the ground started to rise back up again, that told me I knew where I was.

I let out the breath I'd been holding in and stopped a minute to slip off the sack Pearl made up for me and get a good drink. I wet the handkerchief and wiped down my face and combed back my hair with my fingers. There was nothing I could do about the mess on my dress. I knew where the path went next. It would veer off west, around a big stand of poplars, then curve back around and put me at the edge of the back fields at the Marcus place. I put the water jar and handkerchief back in the sack, shouldered into the straps and headed on. I was almost there.

Then I saw one of the big poplars was crashed down across the path. I could see the trunk end from where I stood, the roots all torn up out of the ground. I didn't know what could have made that happen to a tree, maybe it was just old, like the one that tore down the Marcus's fence. I couldn't see the top of the tree, it had fell into a mess of laurel. There was laurel all around that stand of poplar, that's why the path crooked around the way it did, sending you in a big loop out of your way. It took about as long to make that go-around as the whole rest of the walk.

But it wasn't just laurel all around the poplars. That downed tree was covered in poison ivy, all of them were, there wasn't no climbing over it. I couldn't believe it, I just stood there looking at it, like if I looked long enough it would not be so. I'd have to turn and go back.

Or else go straight on, through the laurel.

I knew laurel was serious business. It's a bush, even though it gets as tall as trees in some spots. If you picture a stand of bare trees in winter, just the tree-top part, how the branches look so dense and tangled together you can't see through them—I heard somebody telling stories at the post office once, saying that's what it's like to be inside a laurel hell. It's like trying to walk through something like that. The branches are smaller, he said, but they're all around you, under your feet and over your head.

Almost everybody's got a story about somebody they knew, or their neighbor knew, that got lost in a laurel hell. Sometimes the person gets out, sometimes they don't. There's new stories and old ones both—people coming out half dead or half crazy, or else just never seen again.

I tried to keep a cool head, but I needed to keep walking. I didn't know if I was trying to walk away, or to, or through. I felt in my body right then, how Aunt Hesty must have felt all the times I'd heard her say she needed to walk. I walked back around the bend and stood looking into the laurel, back to look at the tree again, back to the laurel. It didn't look so thick, there on the edge. I tried to remember the map in the post office in Paintsville, and it seemed to me the Marcus back field wasn't but a quarter mile or less straight ahead from where I was standing.

Everybody said to don't even think about it. Daddy would say all the time, "Keep a cool head, Linney."

I turned myself around to head back home and everything started roiling around inside me.

They would want Robbie back, of course they would. They would let me go. If Pearl had let Robbie go, why not me?

That was still the deal. I would have to go back home. And they would never make room for me to be anything other than what I'd always been in that house. Captured, is what I'd be.

No. I am not doing that.

I thought I would throw up when I heard myself think those words. Like I could say what was a done deal and what was not.

My head was hot. Everything that had made me mad or hurt my feelings or scared me since the day all this started gathered itself on the path back the way I'd come and swarmed all over me like the poison ivy over those poplars. I squatted down, wrapped my arms around my knees and cried.

That's where Daddy's cool head got me, falling down in the road and crying.

But just for a minute. I stood up and shook my head to clear it. I pressed the heels of my hands against my eyes to stop crying.

There was no path to follow, not the way I thought there would be. And I could not go back the way I came. I had to know some things for myself. I had to find out what I was going to do about it all.

It wasn't about getting to Delsie anymore, needing somebody else's ears to be able to hear myself. The laurel had tripped me up long enough for everything, my whole story, everything I was afraid of, to catch up with me.

When I looked at the laurel hell, I was looking at the shape of my life. I couldn't go back from it, I had to go through.

It was not so bad at first. I was pretty sure I could go straight, and I could find places to set one foot in front of the other. I could hold open enough space between the branches and twigs to get my body through. It was about a head taller than me for a good while. The laurel was well past its flowering, and while there was leaves on the branch ends and some scattered through, they were mostly gone.

The branches and twigs were bald-looking, the way a woody vine looks. They looked to be the color of dry dirt where the sun was getting through to them.

Some was as skinny around as my little finger, some thick as a man's arm where they come up out of the ground. Except for right there where they was coming out of the ground, all of them looked jointed, twisted, crookedy. Witchy.

"You don't scare me," I said out loud, using my voice to keep going. "I am not stopping for you."

I kept saying that, every place that slowed me down, and there was getting to be more and more such places.

"You don't—" I was raising my left arm up to push a big tangle out of my face when a cluster of little branches and twigs dropped down and hung a few inches from my face right at eye level. I jerked back.

The bigger branch had a knobby end that caused it to crook back into an upside down V-shape. A knuckly twig had caught on it that stuck out straight like a thumb and four spindly twigs sprung back a knot on it and curled up into the V-shape.

It was the shape of my bad hand, exactly.

I stared. I was as scared as if I'd come on a mirror right there in the middle of a laurel hell and seen a wild bad girl that couldn't be me.

I knocked it away quick, but it was too late, it had already grabbed my stomach and give it such a twist I felt wrenched out of myself. When I let go of the tangle I'd been trying to push through, it whipped right back and slapped me across my face.

It caught the corner of my right eye and for a few seconds I couldn't open either eye. I froze, blind and stung and out in the middle of something, a hell way bigger than I'd figured on. My hands shook so bad, I couldn't touch the corner of my eye to see if the skin was cut, or if there was something in my eye. Finally

I thought to put my finger against my cheek to steady it and slide it up to my eye. There was a little drop of blood on it when I pulled it away. The skin stung, but I could blink without it hurting.

I was just scratched. I was just scratched.

I closed my eyes again and took deep breaths, deep like a person who has been running for a long time, or like a person who is fixing to go under for a long swim across a big water. "Please," I said. I didn't know to what.

I opened my eyes. I wanted to know if I could still see the edge of the laurel, where I'd come in. No. The only way to go straight, I'd figured when I started out, was to keep my eyes on my feet and not let them go anywhere but straight ahead, no matter what I had to get through, no matter how much easier it might look to go around some other way. I looked down at my feet and lifted each one up to see if I left a track I could see. No. I wasn't even walking on ground anymore, it was layers and layers of twig and leaf litter. I crouched down and dug through about three or four inches of it with my fingers before I felt solid ground. When I stood back up I twisted around best I could without moving my feet—nothing but laurel, it all looked the same, everywhere I could see.

I wisht I'd thought to blaze a trail, but even if I tried to do that from here on out, I'd never be able to look back and see it in all the broke-looking, tangled mess. I'd lost my sense of time, too, I had no idea how long I'd been inside, how far in I'd gone.

I looked up to see if I could tell anything by the sun, but the laurel had closed in over my head. Best I could tell from looking around me, it had clouded over, for no sun was getting through. It must be afternoon,

I thought, it must be the rain fixing to come on. When I looked back down, around me, still nothing human as far as I could see, only wild, and everything started to look like hands—reaching down, up, across, over. I was trapped, netted, so this was what it meant to be lost.

I heard something move between the ground and the layers of leaf litter.

Nobody was expecting me at the Marcus place.

I wanted to run. I took off, fast as I could go. I forgot to watch my feet. I went crashing through wherever I saw an opening, everything was brittle and dry and it was a terrible racket in my ears that made me feel more lost and strange, but I couldn't slow down.

It crackled and snapped and exploded—what it must sound like to be inside a fire—and I tried to go faster to get out. I tripped and got up, I got snagged, like by a trap wire, across my middle, across my shins and my neck, and fell backwards or forwards. My dress caught on roots sticking up out of the ground, my hair caught on hanging-down claws of twigs. I had bits of leaf and twigs in my hair and in my shoes, but I was afraid to stop and shake them out. There was no end to it, there was no end to it—till I caught both feet on a root or a branch and fell forward full on my face.

It was so mean, it felt so mean, I didn't have anything in me to fight such a thing.

I sat up and felt my face, my mouth felt numb for a second, then it hurt so bad. I pulled my hand back to look. My fingers were bloodied from my mouth, my palm scraped raw. I was sitting in a little nest of dry leaves that had shored up on the other side of the root that had sent me flying.

"Why?" I was asking when I could get my mouth to move.

Nothing answered.

Nothing answered and there was nowhere to go. Every bush coming out of the ground looked like my bad hand just waiting for me to get near enough to grab. I got up on my feet but my legs wouldn't hold me, so I sat back down. I listened for anything moving around, anything that might smell my blood.

I couldn't move, part of me didn't even want to move.

A terrible sleepiness come on me. I was all banged up and all used up every which way, but this was a different kind of sleep than come from being tired, this was a creature, it smelled my blood. It was coming for me.

It was like a tunnel, or something alive down in a tunnel, sucking me down from the inside, down into some kind of mud where I'd never do another thing, take another step, think another thought.

Maybe I didn't have to figure anything out, it said. What was I doing? It was none of it up to me. They would decide, Mama and Daddy, Virgil and Pearl. They had already decided, of course they had, it was done.

I practically felt my eyes roll back in my head, that was how sleepy I was.

I was holding on, though. I had to make it out, I wanted out and I couldn't care what happened to me if I could just make it back out of this terrible hell. My whole body was hurting, seizing up the way it will when you've walked too far and then sat down too long. My face felt scalded, and my palms burned.

There's no need for all this, the thing in the tunnel said, it's too much and anyway you already know how it is.

My head was falling forward and jerking back, the way it does when you're falling asleep in a chair. I started to think maybe I wanted to lay down in that little nest of leaves and slip into that tunnel where none of this was really happening and nothing would ever happen again. I let myself fall onto my side and curl up. I started having little flashes of dream, how I do when I know I'm falling asleep.

And there she was, looking at me, the doe. Just her eyes, so dark, circled with white.

"Linney," a voice said, through the dream. My name in a woman's voice I never heard before, and that was all. My name as clear as day, spoke from somewhere inside my head and that I heard from somewhere that was not my ears.

But it knew me, that voice, it could see me, maybe it even loved me, and I wanted to hold onto it more than I wanted to sleep.

I rolled over onto my back, my face was wet. I pushed myself up onto my elbows.

"I will," I said to the voice.

I was trying to hold on, but already I was forgetting the exact sound of it. "I will," I said again. It took all I had and a little bit more to sit the rest of the way up.

I knew the laurel could win. I knew I might not get out of deals other people made. But it was up to me whether I went to sleep. It was up to me what I said with my own mouth.

I knew there was all kinds of borning and dying, and still there were things I could choose.

"*No,*" I said to the laurel, through the taste of blood in my mouth. "*You* don't say."

It turned out Danny had got so cranky and fidgety about not coming along to see Delsie that Pearl had finally pushed him down off the porch steps herself. "Just go on, then, get out of here," he told me she said. But her and Aunt Hesty told him to walk the wagon road, so at least I could have my walk in peace. He got to the Marcus place a little after dinner time, and that's when they knew something was bad wrong. Him and Mr. Marcus went running up the path through the woods and come on the downed poplar from the other side.

"I told him, I said, 'She gone around, into the laurel,'" Danny said. "He said, surely not, surely you knowed better than that, but I had a bad feeling. I told him you was acting funny this morning, you was not yourself."

Mrs. Marcus and Delsie had put me in one of Delsie's dresses by then and they was all circled around me sitting in a straight back chair in the front room. Mrs. Marcus was wiping off my face, tending to that scratch up by my eye. Delsie was standing behind me, waiting for her mama to get done around my eye to keep combing the mess out of my hair. They was all talking and telling me everything they'd done.

I was glad for them to be talking. For one thing, it was a human sound and my ears felt all scratched up on the inside from hearing myself crash around in the laurel. Maybe I wasn't keeping track of what all they was saying, but whatever it was, it sounded as sweet to me as singing. And for another thing, I didn't have any words yet to tell what it had been like in there.

I said to Danny, but maybe I only whispered it, or imagined I said it out loud, because nobody answered me back, I said, "I am myself now."

"I thought surely you'd turned back," Mr. Marcus said, "and was probably back home by the time Danny got here. We run back here and sent Katie on the horse down to Chandlers' to see, but we couldn't wait to hear. We all of us come back except Ollie, we didn't want her around that laurel at all, she's not got sense enough to be safe. Me and Danny went in a little ways with ropes tied on our belts, hollering for you loud as we could. Kate and Delsie stood on the edge holding the other ends of ropes."

"That didn't work," Danny said. "Hard enough to get yourself through laurel, much less dragging a rope that catches on everything."

"We went in as far as we could and still hear Kate and Delsie hollering at us from the edge," Mr. Marcus went on. "We was just waiting to get word that you wasn't back home already before we went in."

"I wasn't waiting," Danny said, "but I tell you what, you think you can keep track of where you're going but you can't do it. Linney—" he stopped.

"I could hear him," Mr. Marcus said. "I got to him and I liked to had to drug him out, but I told him, I said, we've got to go back out and figure out how to do it and get some help."

Part of me was still lost in there, and when Mr. Marcus said that, about him and Danny going back out without me, I started crying.

Delsie was still standing behind me. She put her hand on my forehead and smoothed my hair back, over and over till I could stop. My face felt so bare, all of them standing around and looking at me while I cried, but there was not a thing I could do about it.

"We knew it'd still be an hour or so before Katie could get back with word," Mr. Marcum picked up the story. "You couldn't pry Danny away, he was pacing at the edge of the hell and hollering for you. He'd have been in there, I know and believe, if it hadn't been Delsie holding him back. I took one of the horses fast as I could go to the Beecham place and they all come back with me. I figured if we all walked in a line across, and none of us lost sight of the next one over, we couldn't get too lost. But before we got back, Delsie got the idea about the dogs."

That was what had saved me. I had dragged myself up out of that little nest of dry leaves but I was so tired and it got so hard to walk standing up straight through the knots of branches I give up and got down on my hands and knees. That made it easier to get through, but something about it made it harder to keep going. I didn't feel like a person, on all fours like that, that's the last thought I remember having in my head. I couldn't think any more about what I should be doing, my arms and legs was doing whatever they did on their own. I didn't know how long that went on.

Then I heard a yelp, like something hurt. I went that way, straight toward anything that was alive like me. It seemed like the sound kept moving without any kind of direction or sense, but I just kept aiming for it and heading wherever it seemed to be. I started to hear another sound, the crackling sounds of it moving through the laurel, so I knew I was getting closer.

I got to where I could tell it was a dog by the sound of the yelp, and then I seen the tail end of it ahead of me. I tried to keep it in sight, it was getting easier to see through the laurel and I begun to think maybe, maybe I would get out.

Then I was out, laying out in the clear with that dog standing over me and barking up a storm. Somebody would come. I laid there looking up at the good brown dog.

"I know you," I said to him. "I know you." It was that dog that had come out to cool off with me and Delsie at the pump, that first time I'd come to the Marcus place.

Danny and Mr. Marcus kept on talking. I heard something about them sending the Beecham boys back home, and Katie still not back. Mrs. Marcus and Delsie was staying right by me, keeping their hands on me. Somebody brought me a plate and a glass of milk.

"Maybe we ought to just keep her the night," Mrs. Marcus said. "Danny, you could go on toward home and meet whoever's on their way here, let them know she's safe but she's all wore out. We can take her home in the wagon in the morning."

"I want to go home." I couldn't not go home.

"Now, Linney," Mrs. Marcus started in.

"Danny," I said, and I lifted my arms up to him, the way a child will do when it wants picked up and carried.

"We'll take a horse," he said, "I'll ride him back first thing in the morning."

I rode in front, with Danny behind so he could hold onto me better. I was so sleepy, I could have slid right off—not that bad, tunnel kind of sleep, but still I wanted to be awake. I was glad it was Danny. He felt older than the others ever since we knew he was getting married. More like Virgil.

"How will you do it?" I asked him. I was tired enough I wasn't clear about what I was saying out loud and what I was only thinking.

"What, honey?" he said.

"Leave."

"Leave what?"

"Home. Pearl."

He didn't answer and I thought maybe I was dreaming, maybe it was one of those morning kinds of dreams where you think you're up and awake and moving around, when the truth is, the dream is just fooling you into staying asleep.

"The time just comes," he said, "and you know it, so there's really nothing else you can do."

We went on a ways, the sound of the horse's hooves on the hard road sounded so good and clear in my ears. He said, "So it's alright. It's alright to leave. You know it when it comes."

I nodded, at least I thought I did.

"What's that?" I raised my head up to hear better, twisted around and tried to see back over Danny's shoulder. He looked around too.

"It's your friend," he said, and it was, the brown dog that had led me out of the laurel was running after us fast as his legs could carry him and barking with what breath he could spare for as fast as he was running. Danny slowed down to where he could catch up with us. Danny tried to shoo him back home, but the dog just sat and looked back and forth between him and me. Danny stopped all the way then, got down off the horse to scoop him up, and hoisted him up in front of me. "I reckon he belongs with you now," he said. "They must have sent him down the road to go home with us."

We hardly fit, the three of us on that horse, but the dog laid half on my lap, half off, his front legs hanging over one side of the horse and his chin flat on one of my knees, his hind end and back legs hanging over the other side. Every once in a while, he'd lift his head up enough to look up at me and make sure I wasn't going to make him get off. I was not.

"I got you a good name for him," Danny said. "Guess."

"I can't guess nothing," I said.

"Serious."

I felt myself lost in the sea of the laurel, all them branches and twigs aimed at me like arrows. I pictured the little dog running back and forth at the edge, crying for me, then coming in after me. Leading me out, staying with me till Delsie and Mrs. Marcus come. How he come running after me still, when it was all over, making sure I got home.

"I don't think so," I said.

"Really? You got something else?"

"I do," I said. "Brother."

Danny drew back for just a second, like it surprised him. "Linney," he said, "I like it."

And then there they all were, down the road in front of us, the horses bringing the wagon toward us as fast as they could with Virgil and Tom up on the seat, Pearl and Aunt Hesty, Doug and Walt and Katie in the back.

Pearl was climbing out the back of the wagon when it got in hearing range, before Virgil got the horses all the way stopped. All of them was grabbing onto me, there was a lot of carrying on and I couldn't really take any of it in. I kept a hold on Brother, Danny hung around the edge, then he worked his way through them all, put his arm around my shoulder and started walking me toward the wagon. "She needs to go home," I heard him tell Pearl. "I'll tell you all about it, just get her in the wagon and let's get her home." So that's what happened. I got in the back of the wagon, Pearl and Aunt Hesty held me and Brother between them. I heard Virgil tell Tom to ride Katie back home on the horse me and Danny was on and walk back home, or else stay the night at Marcus's if it was getting too much on toward dark. Danny sat across from us in the back of the wagon and told them things. I don't remember anything else for sure.

I might have been dreaming when I heard Aunt Hesty say, "Good dog. Such a good dog," then put her mouth right up to my ear and whisper, "I see you got you a Brother."

Way Back When

OVER THE NEXT COUPLE OF WEEKS, I told little bits about the laurel hell. I couldn't answer the first question everybody asked—why did I go in, what was I thinking?

It wasn't about thinking, was all I could say to that. It wasn't just the strangeness of it and how scared I'd been that made it hard to talk about. It was the way my bad hand had dropped down in my face in the shape of that broke-off branch and twigs. It was that creature in the tunnel of sleep that tried to pull me down there with it. The doe and the voice in the dream. I didn't know how to talk about those things any more than I could talk about what happened with me and Aunt Hesty when we went off into the place.

Brother was following me everywhere I went. Pearl let him lay under the table while we cooked so he wouldn't be underfoot, and she said he could sleep in my room, just not in my bed, please. "Good dog," Aunt Hesty bent over to pet his head all through the day. "Such a good dog." Pearl and Aunt Hesty watched on me pretty close. Not like I might run off into the laurel again, but like I might be sick.

I was not sick. I was myself, even if I didn't know hardly what that was.

One morning between cleaning up after breakfast and starting dinner the three of us was out on the porch, figuring out about Danny's and Delsie's quilt. They'd finished all the little four-patches and spread them all out on the floorboards to see how to put it all together. They were both in the porch swing, leaning over and looking. I was down on my hands and knees moving the patches around here and there as they pointed and said, "Try that red one next to the blue, not that blue, the other one" and such as that. They agreed on sashing the four-patches with the solid strips. Pearl wanted to sash each one and set them on point, like diamonds. Aunt Hesty wanted to set each four-patch on point with muslin triangles, then sash each block and set them in straight rows. More air in it that way, she said. It was a lot more work that way, though, and time was getting short. There was still the quilting to get done.

"What do you think, Linney?" Aunt Hesty said.

"I like the idea of the muslin," I said, "but won't that take as long as it's took for you to get all the patches done?" I tried to picture it both ways in my head. "And then it'd be so much bigger to get quilted, too."

"I bet we could get Kate and the girls to come down and with all of us we'd have it done in a couple days," Aunt Hesty said.

"Mommy, we are not having Delsie down here to work on her own quilt," Pearl said. "I am not doing that."

I am not doing that. Right out loud, she said it. Like that was a thing a person could say.

"Fine."

"Fine."

"Linney," Pearl said, "you think you can cut us some strips to length? Just match up a good color for each of the patches, lay one edge of the patch on the strip and cut it to size. Cut two to that size, then we'll come back around and cut the longer sides when we've got the shorter sides stitched on."

I could do that, though it was a little bit slow lining up the edges before I cut. I started in while they sat there watching me, waiting to be handed up something to stitch.

"You hurt your hand when you was in there?" Aunt Hesty asked me.

"A little bit, I scraped up my palm but it's not bothering me too much," I said, still holding the scissors, but waving my hand up to where she could see.

"The other one."

I mostly think it's not for other people to talk about my bad hand. I kept my eyes on what I was doing as I lined up the next patch and strip.

"I'm going as fast as I can," I said. I didn't feel nice about it.

"Mommy—" Pearl said, but Aunt Hesty cut her off.

"I seen you been keeping your hand in your pocket again, since you got back. I thought maybe something happened to it." She was looking at me out the corner of her eye, how she does when she thinks something is going on besides what seems to be going on. I felt it all through my body, all over again, scared sick when I seen my own bad hand reaching for me from out of that laurel.

I'd been hunched over the piles of patches and strips, but I sat back flat on the floor when she said that and looked up at her. She knew something. She was knocking on a door and I'd have to open it if I wanted to know what it was she knew.

"There was something," I said. I was searching in my head for some way to tell about that laurel branch grabbing at me, but she didn't wait to hear anything more.

"Way back when," she said, "in a whole other place, there was a girl. Now for a long time, this girl was pretty much left on her own. I don't mean she was out living in the woods, nothing like that, it was more like nobody talked much to her, nor thought much about her. See, her mommy had took sick and died when the girl was about nine or ten, you know, that time when a girl starts turning into who she's going to be. Lord, Pearl, I remember you then—wanting to know about everything from snakes to how to make biscuits and always asking me what was I thinking. Every time I turned around, "What are you thinking now, Mommy?' I'd tell you best I could, and if I couldn't tell you, I'd say, 'What are you thinking right now, Pearl?' Mostly you'd tell me, but every once in a while, you'd tuck your chin down and look up at me and tell me it was a good thing I didn't know. Them's sweet days." She elbowed Pearl, and Pearl smiled down at the sewing in her hands.

"But this girl," Aunt Hesty set down the pieces she'd been sewing on the arm of the porch swing, picked up some more, and went on, "she didn't have her mommy to ask her questions to. Her daddy, now, he wasn't a bad man, but he was one of them that thinks he can just go about his business, doing how he likes, and everything else will just take care of itself. He wasn't careful with people, was the problem with him."

She looked at me full on then, with her eyebrows up, like we both knew what she was talking about. I looked away, out towards the edge of the woods.

"This girl, let's call her Lissa, she did have something to help her, though. When her mommy knew she was going to die, she made a little rag doll for Lissa and she sewed a little dress and apron for it out of the same feedsack she'd made Lissa's own favorite little dress and apron from. She finished it one morning when they was sitting out on the porch and sewing together. She put them little clothes on the doll and she told Lissa, she said, 'Now put her in your apron pocket and keep her there, because that's where she lives, right there with you, all the time. And if you're not sure about something, or you don't know what to do some time, ask her what to do and she'll tell you. You won't hear what she says with your ears, now, you'll hear it from somewhere else and that's how you'll know it's her talking to you.'"

"There's some would call that crazy talk," Aunt Hesty leaned forward toward me, "but I wouldn't be one of them."

"No, ma'am," I said.

"Well, the years went on, as years will do, and whenever Lissa had trouble, or whenever she was lonely, she'd put her hand in her apron pocket and hold on to that little doll and wait for help, which always come to her, every time. And for the daddy too, the years went on, as years will do, and he met a woman just like him and fell in love and married. She had two daughters just like her, so now Lissa was living in a whole house full of people that figured they could be about their business, doing whatever they wanted, and everything else would take care of itself—by which they meant, Lissa would do it. Now, by nature, Lissa was a good girl."

I looked up quick at Aunt Hesty from the strips I was going along cutting while she was telling the story. "That's right," she said, nodding at me in a way that reminded me of that morning in the kitchen when she was singing her "Jesus Loves Me" song without the words. Like I knew exactly what she was talking about.

"Good. Now, it's hard to bother people that know they're going to do whatever they want no matter what, but you know what really rankles them? Somebody that's good, good down in their heart, all the way down in their bones. So it didn't take long for that woman and her girls to turn on Lissa, not just making her do everything but being real mean about it too. Pretty soon they got so hateful, they started trying to figure out some way to get rid of her."

"Now, Pearl, I don't know if you remember this or not, but when we first were living up here in Kentucky, and when you was still pretty little, lots of things was hard to come by. Like matches, they wasn't even in the little store here when me and Will first come. You had to keep a fire going in the stove or in the fireplace all the time. If you let it go out, you'd have to do that business with the sticks or with a flint, but if it was wet outside you might have a problem. So people would borrow fire, that's what they called it, borrowing fire. They'd send one of the children with a covered pot over to the neighbors, if there was neighbors, for a few red hot coals to get their fire going again."

"That woman and them girls, what they did was, while the daddy was off hunting, they let the fire go out. Their closest neighbor lived so far away, they'd never even met her, only heard tell she was a granny woman—some said a witchy woman—that lived in a little shack on the creek way on the other side of the woods. 'You have to go, or else we'll all freeze' they told Lissa, for it was way down in the fall. They give her a little iron pot and sent her out walking into the woods after supper with no more directions than to follow the creek till she come on that little shack."

I could feel my mouth tightening up. It felt good to cut with the scissors.

"Reach me up something red to stitch on, Linney," Aunt Hesty leaned over and looked at the piles of patches and strips for a minute before she went on. "I'm tired of looking at brown and blue. Anyway, Lissa sets out walking alongside the creek, it's getting darker and darker and her with no light to see by except the moon. On and on she goes, getting scareder by the minute, because who wouldn't, till she sees a shape ahead of her that looks bigger and darker than all the other dark shapes around her. It's the granny woman's shack. She hears a creaky sound, which is that old granny woman rocking on her rocking chair out on the porch, waiting for Lissa like she knowed she was coming.

'Girl,' she hollers out from the porch, 'what's your business here?' Lissa puts her hand on the doll in her apron pocket and waits to hear what to answer.

'I have a need,' she tells the granny woman.'"

I don't know why, but tears come on me, hearing that. I rubbed my face with my shoulder quick, and kept cutting and piling, patches and strips.

"The granny woman tells her to come on then. 'I got needs too,' she tells Lissa. She shows her a big mess of dishes and pots and pans on the table—there wasn't a thing in that shack a body could cook in or eat off of that was clean. Black grease cooked onto the frying pans an inch thick, burnt beans in the pots, the kind of mess it takes years to make. Stink like you wouldn't believe. 'You help me, maybe I'll help you,' the granny woman says.

Well, Lissa, she'd done plenty of dishes and cleaned up some pretty tall messes in her time, but this was a whole other thing. She put her hand in her apron pocket to see what her doll said about it. 'Just start' was the word that came, so she did. She scraped and scoured all night long and come morning she was about half done."

"It wasn't all done?" I asked, for everybody knows that by morning, whatever it is, it's always all done.

"This is for real, Linney," Aunt Hesty said. "It was about half done. The granny woman, she sniffed, and harrumphed and poked around at things with her stick. 'I'll give you another try,' she says, and she points over at a big pile of clothes and house things to wash. There was not a clean dress nor apron in the house for a body to put on, not a rag nor towel but what would make things dirtier than how they started out. I mean, it was foul. Same thing as before—'Just start' from the doll, so Lissa works all night building a fire and boiling and scrubbing and come morning it's about half done.

'One more try,' the old woman says again and she takes Lissa out to the barn and shows her a big pile of corn cobs, all chewed on by who knows what, wormy, and all kinds of nastiness on it, and she wants all the good kernels picked out and washed and ready to mill by sunup. Lisa's starting to get a little edgy by now, because who wouldn't, and tired and hungry. She puts her hand down in her apron pocket.

'Say no,' she hears."

"'Well, that's about the scariest thing she ever heard. She didn't tell people no—all her life she'd been doing everything people told her to do, right up to her stepmother and stepsisters sending her out into the dark woods at the edge of night with no light nor directions nor nothing, and all her life people had been saying how good she was to be doing that way. Besides, they were counting on her to bring home the fire that would keep them alive, didn't she have to do whatever the granny woman said?"

"She put her hand around the doll again while the granny woman stood there in front of that big pile of wormy corn cobs tapping her foot. 'No,' again."

"So Lissa says 'No' to the granny woman. And soon as she says it out loud, something starts happening. She starts to shake, for she feels like she's stepped off across some kind of threshold into a whole other world, like there's no ground under her feet, and at first she thinks what's happened is, she's done bad."

I wasn't feeling too steady myself. I put the scissors down and pretended to be sorting through the patches and strips to find some good pairs.

"She had crossed over into something new," Aunt Hesty went on, "and that was just what the granny woman had been waiting for."

"Lissa looked around at where she was, thought about the night scouring and scraping, and the night scrubbing and boiling."

"'This mess,' she says to the old woman, 'took years to make. Nobody could clean this up in one night.'"

"She felt like she was waking up out of bad dream. She looked at the mess of corn cobs in the ratty old wormy old barn and 'No,' she says. 'I am not doing that. I'll do my own work,' she says."

"'Well, get on with you then,' the granny woman says, but before Lissa heads out, they go into the old woman's shack and the old woman fills up her pot with hot coals."

"Now, there's some says Lissa went back home and give her stepmother the fire, but the granny woman's fire burned up their cottage and everybody in it."

I felt every hair on my body stand up.

"Some says Lissa was the only one got out. And there's some says Lissa never went back home at all, she just kept walking up the creek till she come on a little village and she went to sewing dresses, and whenever she sewed a dress for a little girl, she made a little doll to go in the pocket. Take your pick," Aunt Hesty said. "It's up to you how it ends."

"But what does it mean, Aunt Hesty?"

"Well, what do you keep in your pocket?" Aunt Hesty asked.

I didn't like to say it out loud. "You know."

"You got to say it," she said.

"My bad hand," I said, half mad. But if we were going to talk about it, I figured I might as well tell it true. "My bad parts," I said.

"Linney, what is bad about a hand?" she asked me. "I ain't asking about hard, I'm asking about bad."

I couldn't say anything. Pearl started to say something, but Aunt Hesty shook her head no at her, without taking her eyes off me.

"What happened in the laurel?"

I told them I knew it was wrong to go in the laurel, I knew what everybody would say about it. I knew it would worry people, it would make trouble, I knew it was a bad idea. I knew I wasn't doing what I'd been told.

"But I had to do it," I said.

"So you listened to your bad part," Aunt Hesty said, but she said 'bad' like it meant something else altogether. "What happened next?"

"That laurel wanted me," I said. "It almost got me."

"What stopped it?"

"I told it no." I could hear how foolish that sounded, even though I knew it wasn't. Aunt Hesty just nodded. "Then Brother found me," I said.

"You alright?"

"Yes."

"Different?"

I let that word pass through me. "Yes," I said.

"Sorry?"

"No," I said. I shook my head. I wiped down my face with both hands like I was getting something off it, then let my hands fall down in my lap and lifted up my face to her. "I can't be sorry."

Aunt Hesty leaned toward me, to where her face was even with mine. "How is that bad, Linney? There's no such thing as a bad hand, that hand, it's just got a different job, something else to teach you besides what your mama told you was good—" when Aunt Hesty said that, Pearl tried to break in with something about my mama loving me, but right then that was not what I needed.

"Your other hand that you hide, your other parts you're not used to listening to, you listened to them, that's all. You went into the laurel, and you come out with something you really needed, ain't that so?" I nodded. "You got your own voice inside you now to tell you what you need to know. It's your own heart you follow now, you let your own heart and your own hands—both of them—tell you what's good for you."

I looked up at Pearl and Aunt Hesty, sitting beside each other on the porch swing, their eyes on me like they had nothing else in the world to think about but whatever I might say next.

I knew what was good when I seen it. I knew I didn't want to go back home to live. I belonged here, with them, all of them.

But there was things I still was worried about—something in me still didn't trust the idea of getting what I wanted.

I didn't want to be like Betts. I wanted to be the kind of girl that would take the fire back home in Aunt Hesty's story. And I still had that question in me about Pearl letting Robbie go.

"I don't know yet," I said, but I held their eyes as I said it. "I still don't know what all of it means."

"You know," Aunt Hesty said, twice jabbing her long crooked finger in my direction, then leaning back again like everything was settled. "You already know, is what it means."

When I went to bed that night, I had Robbie on my heart. We'd not heard back from him after the last letters we sent, me and Pearl. The wedding was just a few weeks away and I was getting worried Daddy was trying to keep him from making the trip home for it. I had Aunt Hesty's story buzzing around in me, so I begun to wonder too, if anything was happening to Robbie like was happening to me.

There wasn't much time for sitting and thinking about things, though. Pearl and Aunt Hesty had got Danny's and Delsie's quilt top together and set up the quilting frame in the front room. If they were going to make it in time for the wedding, they needed every second at it they could get. That meant I was working faster and harder at everything I helped with, always trying to get to where at least one of them could go off and work on the quilt. Pearl had figured out how many rows of blocks they had to get done each week to keep a pace for the wedding.

"We are not going to make it," she said about two weeks before the wedding. I was still in the kitchen sweeping up after breakfast, her and Aunt Hesty had been sitting out there at it for about half an hour. They both of them let their arms fall down at their sides and leaned back from the edge of the quilt frame and looked at each other. They were sitting on the same side of the frame, like people sitting beside each other at a kitchen table, but on opposite ends and working toward meeting each other in the middle. The frame was a big one, eight or nine feet long, trestles on each end a good three feet wide. The quilt went the whole length and you could see, looking where each side of the quilt was rolled up onto the take-up bars that set into notches in the trestles, that they were only about halfway there. I stood in the doorway of the kitchen leaning on the broom and looked at them while they looked at the quilt and each other and tried to figure what to do about it.

"We wanted to do all that canning, too," Pearl said.

"Linney's going to have to help," Aunt Hesty looked up at me and I couldn't figure why she had to look so determined about it, because of course I would help.

"I'll get the water boiling and get the jars out of the cellar and start washing," I said.

"No," Aunt Hesty said. "With the quilt."

"Why not?" she said when I didn't answer, just stood there trying to figure out what she was up to. "You going to tell me you got a bad hand?"

"No, ma'am," I said, but I didn't like it.

She told me to pull one of the kitchen chairs over to the frame beside her. Pearl moved over to the other side, across from where Aunt Hesty put me, and started working from there. I looked over at her a couple of times, thinking it didn't make any sense and that any second now she'd put a stop to it, but she kept her head down.

"You got your topside hand," Aunt Hesty said, and she showed me how she held the needle and rocked it through the layers, her thumb out in front and wiggling the needle with her long middle finger. "And you got your underneath hand. Now all it does is let you know when you've got through all the layers, when the needle hits it, it just pushes it right back up. See, now," she said, and she turned that hand so my wrist was up, "you don't need it to be straight, nor quick, nor nothing, just put a thimble on that longest finger and you got a perfect underneath hand. It knows what to do all on its own, you don't even need to see it. It's like the left hand in the Bible—the right hand knows not what it's doing, but it's doing just fine without the right hand knowing a thing about it." Then she looked at me sideways, how she does.

"Yes, ma'am," I said.

She threaded me up a needle to start. They were stitching lines in Xs across the four-patches and a couple of wavy lines that criss-crossed each other like cables of a rope in the sashing. Mama wasn't much for making quilts, and when she did, she always just tied them, making little knots of yarn through the layers to hold them together. Her quilts were nothing like this. I was scared at first, mostly that I might ruin the wedding quilt, but Pearl said one of the good things about quilts was, they had so many stitches in them, you couldn't really notice when any one of them was crooked. So don't worry, she said, the thing about quilts was to just keep going.

Once I got started, I wanted to keep going. I couldn't say why it felt so good. I got faster and faster.

"How many stitches you got on that needle, Linney?" Aunt Hesty asked me when she was standing up for a minute to stretch her back and get a cup of coffee. That's part of how you go fast—load up the needle with as many stitches as you can before you pull it through. I looked down to see and counted the little bumps of cloth lined up on the needle.

"Eight," I said.

"She's giving you a run for your money, Pearl," Aunt Hesty said.

"Well, good," Pearl said. "Running's just what we need."

By the time we had to stop and start on dinner, my back was beginning to burn between my shoulder blades, but I still didn't want to stop. I had a happiness coming up in me from someplace I'd never been happy before and I couldn't stop smiling. I kept looking over at the quilt and walking over there to run my hands over it. I seen Pearl and Aunt Hesty smiling at each other over me doing that, but I didn't care.

I was working on that quilt with my own two hands. I stretched out my arms and twisted them, wrists up, wrists down. Two hands. One, two. Two good hands.

Robbie's letters come a few days later. It was Mr. Marcus coming back up from Paintsville that brought them to us. He'd been down there with a list of things Mrs. Marcus was wanting for the wedding. The back of their wagon had some boxes and bags in it, things for the new little family, he said, and some sacks of coffee and sugar and white flour.

I felt something strange open up inside me when I heard him say "new little family." I wasn't thinking about getting married, it wasn't like that, but it struck me just then that I was old enough for it. Delsie and Danny was getting married, and I was right behind them. But I had Robbie's letter in my hand, and I let that thought go till I could be alone and quiet with it. I went out on the back porch, Pearl and Aunt Hesty got them some coffee and sat down beside each other at the kitchen table to read theirs. It had been a long time, maybe a couple months since we'd heard from Robbie. So much happened to me in that time, I was almost scared to hear what was happening to him.

September 8, 1910

Dear Linney,

I am counting down the days till I get to come home and see everybody. I think it will be alright this time—surely we'll be done here by the middle of October, so it will just be a matter of a few weeks after the wedding till I can come home to stay. I have to tell you something, Linney, though probably you already seen it coming. Your daddy is talking like we will be doing this same thing again next year, like it's already decided. Have you been hearing any talk like that? When he starts in on what me and him are going to do next year, your mama gives him the bad eye, and once or twice I heard her say "We'll see about that" or some such. But you can tell by his face it's already next year in his head and me and him are out there clearing and planting all over again. Linney, what do you say about that?

Here's what I say. I am not the same as I was when I come here. I never worked so hard nor so long in my life. Now, I'm not all the way sorry for that, though there was plenty of times I felt pretty sorry while I was doing it.

I know I can do it. I know I can do what needs done and get up the next morning and do it again. Maybe if I wasn't here all by myself—without my brothers, is what I mean, because with all of us to pitch in you'd always know that things would get done one way or another—it might have took me a lot longer to know that.

But I figure if I can work like that, I am a man and I can say where I work and where I don't.

One morning I'd got up early to go down to the river before breakfast, how I told you I do sometimes to get some quiet. I'd just got settled in when your daddy come out of nowhere, seemed like, and sat down beside me. "Lord, I wish I could do that," he says, nodding his head at my fishing pole. Long as I been here, that was the first real thing he ever said to me.

"Why don't you?" I asked him. "Waste of daylight," he tells me, and he's already standing back up, hardly sat down long enough to get the seat of his pants dirty. He stood there a minute looking out at the river, and it was pretty that morning,

full green and the sun shining on it. "You always pay for it," he says. Says he can hear his own daddy whenever he slows down, clear as day, telling him he'll be sorry later. They come through the War, his mama and daddy, he says. He says, "You go through days you don't eat, you know what it means, being sorry later."

He kept turning like he was leaving, but he talked a little more. Said he had a baby brother that died a couple years after the War. His mama only ate what him and the other boys left on their plates. He was little and didn't catch on, so he cleaned his plate every time. One of his brothers told the story some years later, when your daddy was ten or twelve or so—it wasn't enough food for his mama, and she lost her milk and the baby died. "So I learned about sorry early on," he says. "Once I got grown, I made it my business to not never be sorry like that again." Then he shakes his hands like he's shaking something off, runs his fingers back through his hair, says, "Daylight's wasting," and he does leave.

I didn't follow after him, though, Linney. That's a terrible story he's got, and from what I can see, he's just keeping it going, how he never looks to nothing but 'later' and 'sorry.' I'm here now and I'll stick it out, but I am not willing to go on like this, doing like him.

I am not the boy that punched my daddy in the stomach and run off, is what I'm saying. Maybe I'm not a grown man, but I have worked like one and if they come at me again with this, I am aiming to stand my ground and tell them—I am not doing that.

That's my most important thing I had to tell you, Linney. Who knows if we will get much of a chance

*to talk by ourselves with the wedding business going
on and all. Right now, we are all of us planning to
come, though your daddy is starting to make noises
about it being a bad time. First time he brought it
up, I said straight away, "I am going to Danny's
wedding." Then he started talking about did I know
how to drive the wagon, and having me load fodder
and drive it on the wagon to the barn to see how I
did. So don't be surprised if he don't come, it might
be just me and your mama and Betts.*

*If I was Aunt Hesty, I'd say "Lord have mercy
on my soul," for you know what that trip will be
like with the two of them. I never did hear people
talk how Betts and your mama talk to each other.
Hurts my ears, just thinking about it. But I will be
thinking about seeing you and Mama and Daddy
and all of them, so I don't think they can hurt my
ears that much. I wish it was now.*

love yr. brother,

Robbie

Well.

Between Daddy's story and Robbie being so sure
about things, I couldn't hold a thought in my head.
And I hadn't even thought about all them coming up
for the wedding, but of course they would do that. I
got up and put the letter in my pocket. I took a few
steps down the porch and said to Pearl and Aunt Hesty
through the screen door, "I need to walk." They was
still reading, but Aunt Hesty looked up at me.

"You fixing to go far?" she asked.

"Maybe I'll be gone for a while, but not far," I said.
"I won't lose sight of the house. I'll be back to help
with supper."

"Well, take some water with you," she said. She looked out toward the window, it was clouding up again. "You're liable to get soaked."

I didn't care. I walked out to the path at the edge of the woods, Brother following after me. Virgil and the boys waved and hollered something at me from where they was working out that way. I waved back and kept going. I walked the path along the edge of the woods, but I didn't feel like going in there.

I wanted clear space around me. I wanted it all to come clear. I walked the edges of the fields where nobody was working. I wanted to walk a straight line from here to there, to anywhere.

I walked and walked those same lines like I was trying to wear my own path into the ground and Brother trotted right along with me like it was a job he knew had to get done. We didn't stop till it started to pour.

That night the three of us stayed up late to put in time on the quilt. It was quiet and still around us in the house, though outside the crickets was making a racket like you wouldn't believe. I was working on the Xs fast as I could and it felt good the same way it had felt good to walk those straight lines out in the fields. Even better, seeing as how I had both my hands in on it with the quilt

"Aunt Hesty," I said. I wasn't sure yet what I was going to ask.

"What, Linney?"

"Did you know my daddy before he married my mama?"

"Little bit here and there, is all."

"Did you know his mama and daddy?"

"Only heard tell."

"What?"

"Rough times after the War. Same as everybody. Everybody had terrible stories back then. Some people went soft in the head, some went hard. Your daddy's daddy was a hard man if I remember rightly."

She finished a needleful of thread, made a knot right on top of the quilt top then give the top layer a little jerk up to pop the knot through to the middle where it wouldn't show. I hadn't learned how to do that yet.

"He never talked about him?" she asked while she stretched out an arm's length of thread for a new needleful.

"Not to me," I said. "He died before Mama and Daddy was even married."

"Now, your mama's daddy, he was a different story. You know him at all?"

I shook my head.

"You remember him, Pearl?" Aunt Hesty asked, and Pearl shook her head. She'd been awful quiet since Robbie's letter, and neither of them had said a thing to me about what he'd wrote to them. She wasn't all ragged though, like she'd been after the first letter. I figured she knew this time he'd be home soon enough.

"He was a Williams, the middle boy. David, I think. No, Davis, they called him—Davis Williams, that was him. We were around him some, but I only knew him from after the War and mostly from things Rose would say. He come home without his right arm, spent the rest of his life sitting. Now, him and Marie, that was Rose's mommy, they married before he went off to the War." Aunt Hesty leaned back from the quilt and let out a breath, then bent over the frame to work again.

"That must have been the kind of thing Daddy thought he was saving me from when he wouldn't let me and Robert marry before he went off, I don't know. I don't know what to think about that. Marie, now, she waited on Davis hand and foot. She had to at first, Lord, some of them boys came back in such a state, all broke up every which way. He got to where he could talk, though, and be around people. But he never did do anything more in this world than sit. Marie just kept doing for him, letting him have his way with about just about everything. Maybe he was that broken, but I always had the sense he felt like he ought never be asked for anything ever again, like he was owed, and it was Marie paid the bill. I don't know.

They lived with his family, or else they probably would have starved. They babied him too, bent the whole household out of shape trying to make up for something nobody could make up for. That's how Rose grew up, with him at the center of everything, not to be bothered, not to be worried with nothing. I'd see her trying to be useful to him, all her young years trying to get him to see her, but I don't think that man could feel nothing much past his own needs. So when Carl Stepp come sniffing around—" Pearl kicked Aunt Hesty under the quilt frame, but she kept on going. I wasn't sure I wanted her to. "—thinking she'd be good for him, it's no wonder she took out of there like a shot. Seemed like he was the opposite of her daddy, full of plans, working like a mule, wanting her to do it all with him."

"Is that bad?" I asked.

"No," Aunt Hesty answered. "It's just, well, like I was telling you about working on the quilt—people got a topside and a underneath to them too. Sometimes the topside makes a pretty good cover-up for things that's going on underneath."

"Like how?"

"Like your mama getting away from her own daddy and all his weight was what her topside hand was doing, but then her underneath hand keeps pushing back so she ends up letting your daddy have his way about everything—just like her mama did with her daddy. You learn things," Aunt Hesty said, "you don't even know you're learning. Some people figure it out, some don't."

"I don't know," I said. I didn't like it.

"What don't you know? You're sitting here like your daddy wanted, ain't you?" Aunt Hesty said. In my head, I heard Delsie saying "ouch" when I was telling her about Betts and Mama and Daddy.

"Let Linney be, Mommy," Pearl said.

"She asked."

"Well, a body can only take so much looking at the underneath of things in a day. Even a quilt," she said. "Come on now, if we don't call it a night, we won't be good for nothing all day tomorrow."

I wove my needle into the quilt and helped Pearl push the frame back out of the center of the room. When I turned around, Aunt Hesty had already gone on into her room. I was so tired my whole body was buzzing, Mama's and Daddy's stories like bees swarming inside me, crazing to get out.

That night I dreamed I moved, all by myself, into a house everybody knew was haunted. It was daytime in the dream, so I wasn't scared though I knew I ought to be. It was a big, fine house, I knew that even though

I was only in the kitchen-but at the same time it felt like it might be the house of that granny woman in Aunt Hesty's story. On the walls of the kitchen it was all chests of drawers, like you'd have in a bedroom, not shelves or cupboards like belong in a kitchen. They went all the way up to the ceiling. I pulled one drawer open, about chest high, and looked in. It was empty. Only thing in it was men's names carved into the sides and bottom of the insides of the drawer, which was a raw, light-colored wood. Not just carved in, the names, but burnt in, like they'd took a tiny red hot poker and wrote with it. They was scattered, dozens of them, and fancy-looking like if you was signing your name to something important. Some was newer and some was older, even three hundred years old. I closed that drawer and opened another one—same thing. I closed that one and turned to where I could see all those empty drawers, all around me. I maybe liked the idea of having so many empty drawers to put things in, but how was I to feed myself in a kitchen as empty as that?

Next morning, I tried to remember some of the names inside those drawers, but I couldn't. I couldn't shake the feeling of the dream either, a feeling like it meant two opposite things at the same time—that all my drawers was empty and I could starve, that all the drawers was mine to fill and that was good.

Over the next few days, though, we got real busy. Robbie and them would come here to stay the night before the wedding and the night after, so Pearl was wanting to get ready for all that company, and finish the quilt, and get that canning done for Danny and Delsie too.

"Let's can some batches in the morning and after supper when it's cooler," Pearl said. The three of us was sitting at the kitchen table after breakfast, gathering ourselves for the day. "And quilt and clean in the in-between."

"Maybe Aunt Hesty can quilt while we do the canning," I said, for she was looking pretty ragged around the edges, and getting crankier by the minute. It was a lot, what we was trying to get done. The canning part was like to kill us.

"Good thinking," Pearl said, and we all sat there, shoulders sagging and looking at each other in case there was anything else we could think of to say that might keep us sitting there resting for just another minute. "When the boys come in for dinner, I'll have one of them to carry us up the jars out of the cellar and set them on the worktable so we can start in the morning."

"The big pot, too," Aunt Hesty said. "And we'll likely need some extra stove wood."

Pearl slapped her hands down on the table. "If we don't start moving now, we never will. How you holding up, Mommy, you want to work on the quilt while me and Linney clean up in here?"

"You know, Pearl," Aunt Hesty said, kind of testy, "it's not the end of the world if we don't get that quilt done by their wedding day. You think either one of them's thinking about what kind of quilt their going to have on their bed that night? That what you and Virgil had on your young minds?"

Pearl said something scolding, but I'd quit listening and gone into the front room to run my hands over the quilt again. I was almost glad for how much work there was. If I filled up enough empty jars, to help fill up Danny's and Delsie's cupboards, maybe I'd know something about what those empty drawers in my dream was trying to tell me.

And right then, I'd rather carry boiling hot jars across the kitchen than Mama's and Daddy's stories in my head. After sleeping on it I knew that much. It was easier to think about not going back home when I was just plain mad at them—at Daddy for coming up with the idea of sending me off in the first place, and at Mama for not telling him no. Now here was this voice in my head telling me it wasn't their fault, that nothing was the way I'd thought, I was wrong about it all. What, really, had they done that was so bad, weren't their stories so much worse than anything that had happened to me? I was just feeling sorry for myself, what in the world could I be thinking?

I recognized that voice, though. It was not the voice from the apron pocket, but the other one, the one from that tunnel of sleep inside the laurel that wanted me to just lay down and close my eyes.

I couldn't have been standing there by the quilt very long when I heard Brother's toenails tapping across the floor toward me. He nosed my hand and whimpered, but I couldn't quite pull myself out of the daze that voice was spinning all around me. Then he yelped like he did in the laurel and nipped at my ankle till I woke out of it and looked down at him. Aunt Hesty was walking by just then. "Good dog," she said and leaned down to pat his head, but she was looking up at me. "Such a good dog."

WEDDING DAY

THE MORNING OF THE WEDDING, Aunt Hesty didn't come out to help with breakfast. We didn't think nothing of it, me and Pearl, for in the last few days we'd all of us worked ourselves down to our finger bones. It was all done, though—the quilt, the jars set into four crates with straw packed in around to keep them safe on the ride to the Marcus place. The three of us had stayed up way into the night for three nights in a row to finish the quilt.

Come to find out, my new hand was shaped perfectly for holding onto the edge of the quilt with the binding folded over it to be stitched down, and my right hand had got real fast. Aunt Hesty slept in the chair while Pearl and I started working on the binding on opposite corners and I did most of three sides. Tired as I was, it felt so good to be in on the quilt for Danny and Delsie, but also on account of it making Pearl so happy to get finished in time for the wedding. When we got done, Pearl and I took a corner of the quilt in each hand to fold it, and we stood apart with it all spread out between us there for a minute, looking at it.

"This is Danny's wedding quilt," she said, and she gave me her full eyes so I could see what a wonder it was that she would be saying such a thing.

"And I helped," I said, and I gave her my full eyes too.

We walked to each other then, with our hands out and up, bringing the corners of the quilt together to fold it. She took the corners out of my hand and folded them in, I picked up the new bottom fold and we did it again. It was pretty as a dance. When it was all folded up, she set it on the chair and we both of us looked and loved on it again before we looked back up at each other.

"I just might be too tired to sleep," Pearl said.

"Not me." I was feeling my eyes beginning to roll back in my head, I was so sleepy all of a sudden.

"Should we wake Mommy up and get her to bed, or just let her stay there in the chair, she looks pretty good there."

"I bet she'll wake up and wander on in when she's ready," I said. "She don't look like somebody that wants waked up." And she didn't. She'd pulled her feet up under her and found a way to lay across the chair so that it looked as cozy as a bed. Pearl got down and kissed her on the face, and she didn't make a move, so we left her and went on to bed.

Come morning, Pearl was so happy while we was making breakfast, you'd never know we'd only slept two or three hours. It was partly the wedding and partly because Robbie was home. He'd come in about the middle of the day before. Turned out he'd come alone. Daddy'd said he couldn't leave, just like Robbie figured he would. He was worried about the fields down close by the river.

This is the problem with bottomland. It's good how it holds the rain and the good dirt, unless there's too much rain, then it's got nowhere to drain. The river was high too, Robbie said, and Daddy was going down there watching on it every hour or so, afraid it was going to come out over its banks. Things being how they was, Mama wouldn't leave him there alone, so they'd sent Robbie up by himself in the wagon. I was partly relieved and partly set to hold it against them that they wouldn't come and see me when they could. "He tried to tell me I couldn't leave, he might need me," Robbie told us, "but it don't matter how many men you have, if a field's going to flood, there's not a thing in the world you can do about it."

"Anyway, I'm here now," he said. He looked all around at all of us, how we'd all come running when we seen him coming in. It was a lot of grinning. Virgil was standing next to Pearl with his arm around her shoulder and he kept squeezing her to him then letting her go, like he was realizing all of a sudden and over and over how happy he was. She was looking at Robbie though, and every once in a while looking around at all of them there together. She looked stunned almost and when I seen her looking at Danny, it come through me almost like a rush of water, what Aunt Hesty always said about there being all kinds of borning and all kinds of dying. I looked over to her real quick and she was watching Pearl too. She looked back at me, those eyebrows up, and I nodded. We would take care of Pearl. We would.

We planned to start out for the Marcus place pretty much at the crack of dawn. The wedding wasn't to happen till just before suppertime, but we wanted to help get everything ready. We'd need time to get ourselves cleaned up after that, and me and Pearl and Aunt Hesty wanted to be there for helping Delsie get ready. Back in the summer, Pearl had helped me make a new dress for the wedding. It was feedsack, but it was the lightest pink, and printed with darker pink dogwood blossoms. We made it with a round neck cut just a tiny bit lower than I'd ever had, no collar, and gathered the neckline a little so it fell so nice to my waist. The waist was fitted. No bow in back, Pearl said, for I was not a little girl. We put an extra panel in the skirt so that it swished around my knees when I walked. It made me feel like I felt the day Aunt Hesty called us beautiful, and I wasn't even the bride. I couldn't imagine how it must feel for Delsie.

Virgil and Pearl had woke up while it was still dark and Virgil had gone around and knocked on all the bedroom doors, saying Wedding day, Wedding day, to get everybody up.

Everybody was at the breakfast table but Aunt Hesty. Pearl sent Robbie to get her up.

"We was up till all hours," she said. "If you go, she won't be so cranky about it."

We heard him open her door, but there wasn't any talking. I looked over at Pearl. I had a bad feeling. She was looking to Virgil, and he was moving fast toward Aunt Hesty's room.

It felt like one of those moments when you're about to fall and you know it, or else you've spilled something hot across your hand and it's the half-second before the burning sets in.

"She's not here," I heard Robbie say. That wasn't exactly what I was afraid I'd hear, so it took a second for my ears and my head to get together and try to make sense of it. Pearl was standing up, working her way around the table to get to the back room. "Her bed's not even slept in," Robbie said.

"She was sleeping in the chair when we got done with the quilt," Pearl said. "We thought we'd best not wake her." Her and Virgil looked at each other without saying a word.

"We'll all of us have to go looking," he said. The boys was all standing around them by then. "Start close by the house and work your way out. Come back to the house about every hour so we can keep figuring out what to do if we need to. Walt," he said, "you ride out to Marcus's right now and tell them Aunt Hesty's not feeling quite right and we'll just be a little later than we thought. Tell them noontime, and if we have to change it we will. Stay here at the house when you get back, in case she makes her way back here." Then he pointed the boys all in different directions, to look. "Take whatever breakfast you can carry," he said, "and some water, we don't know what kind of shape she'll be in when we find her."

"We'll find her," he said to Pearl. "We always do."

"Me and Linney are going looking too," Pearl told him. "Don't worry if it takes us a little bit longer to get back in."

The boys grabbed what they could carry off the table and some of the extra jars we'd left sitting on the worktable to fill up out at the pump. They looked like they'd done this kind of thing before, though I'd not seen anything like this. I was standing still in the middle of the kitchen feeling them all moving so fast around me. Pearl come up behind me.

"Linney," she said, and she give me a little shake on my shoulder. "You alright?" She shook me again. "I need you, Linney."

I turned around and the look in her eyes, like there was only the one thing that mattered in the whole world that morning, woke me up. "What?" I asked.

"It's maybe the wedding," she said. "This happened when me and Virgil got married, even way back then when Mommy was still right as rain. I'll tell you, but we've got to get going because there's no telling what she might get into now, out there by herself." Pearl had been pacing around, picking up food and tying it up into a cloth. "Pick up a couple jars," she said, "we'll fill them up on our way out." She stopped then and looked at me to make sure I was hearing her. I was. I had the jars in my hands and I'd got out the little sack with the shoulder straps I had with me when I got lost in the laurel, to carry the water jars in.

"It's been a long time since I been there," she said. "I'm not sure."

"I don't know—" I didn't know what she was saying.

"The place," she said. "She took you there, didn't she? That day?"

Of course. The borning and the dying. The wedding. Of course.

"I didn't pay hardly any attention," I said, "I was trying so hard to keep up with her." I was trying right then to keep up with Pearl. She was already halfway down the porch steps.

"Between us, we ought to be able to get there," Pearl said, without looking back at me. She stopped at the pump and reached for the first of the jars I was carrying and while she was pumping with one hand as fast as she could and holding the jar underneath with the other, she looked up at me. "We have to."

We could hear Virgil and the boys calling Aunt Hesty, Aunt Hesty, from places nearer and farther, from all four corners of the farm. "We will," I said. She held up the filled jar. I gave her the other one and used both my hands to screw the lid down on the full one and set it down into the little shoulder sack. They made a little clinking noise behind me at every step as we set out at a half-trot to get to the edge of the woods.

We couldn't walk so fast in the woods. A few leaves had started to come down, which made it harder to see the path, and the rain had made them slick. I had a sense of what direction to go in, and when to begin to curve around, but it was pretty fuzzy. Pearl, on the other hand, seemed to know some of the signs, to recognize some of the trees I remembered Aunt Hesty putting her hands on to get her bearings when she'd brought me this way.

"I was out here the morning of my wedding day," Pearl said, after a long time of neither of us speaking a word except to point out what we thought was the way. I didn't ask any questions, I wanted to know what she wanted to tell me.

"I was so mad." She stopped. I almost run into her. "I hope Danny's not mad."

"Not Danny," I said. I was sure. That seemed to be good enough for Pearl.

"All my life," she said, "it was me and Mommy— Uncle Will was there too, but he was always a little bit off to the side. She didn't much like it when Virgil come along. I thought she'd run off that morning to try to stop me marrying him and leaving her. Thing is, we weren't even leaving, we was planning all along to live on right here with her and Uncle Will. Lord knows, she never done anything like that before. At all. It was always the opposite, always felt like she was right on top of me."

That's not so bad, I thought, but I didn't say.

"I'd only been up here twice. Same as you, the first time, and a little bit after I knew I was going to marry Virgil, for that talk." Pearl looked at me then, like maybe she shouldn't have said that. I could feel my face heat up.

"I won't be needing that talk," I said.

"Well, good, that's just as well," Pearl said, and went back on with her story. "It was the only place I knew of she might come to that was away from me." Pearl stopped and held back a mess of greenbrier that had grown up and arched across the path like a bridge, so I could get through without getting all tore up. It whipped back when she let it go and then she started up her telling again. "I was right, there she was. Sitting on the rock outside the cave, looking about as lone and lorn as a soul could look. It was my wedding day, now, and I wasn't of a mind to be feeling sorry for her. I thought she was just being pitiful to get me to change my mind, or just to spoil it for me. I never seen her act like that, but like I keep saying, it was my wedding day and I needed things to be right, I needed her and me to be right."

We got stopped right then by a big puddle, almost as wide as a little creek, across the path. "Which way do you think?" Pearl asked, as we looked to the left and to the right to see the best way around. We went around to the left, it didn't take us out of sight of the path. When we got back on the path, I wasn't sure. "Does this look right to you?" I asked Pearl. I had to ask it again, for she was already down the way quite a bit. "We've got to hurry it up," she said, and just then I felt under my feet how the ground was starting to rise. "I think we're close," I said. "It's getting harder to walk."

I thought she was done talking and fixed on getting to the Place quick as we could.

"Anyway," she said, over her shoulder, for the path was getting narrow and I was having a little trouble keeping up, "that wasn't it at all."

We come around a little bend, and there was the hillside. We stood still, the two of us there, looking up there to see what we could see, and I could feel the quiet again, the way I'd felt it before.

"There she is," Pearl said, and she put her hands on either side of my face and turned it so I could find Aunt Hesty with my eyes. She was out on the rock, we could only just see the top of her head from where we was standing at the bottom of the hillrise. I headed up there as directly as I could see to go. I heard Pearl let out a breath and start out half a step behind me.

We slowed way down when we got up there where she was. She didn't hardly move, like she knew we was there, but even turning her head would be too much. I looked at Pearl for what to do. "You go to her," she said.

I walked slow the few steps it took me to get close to her where she was sitting right at the mouth of the cave. I was coming from the side. "Aunt Hesty," I said when I got right next to her, then I put my hand—my underneath hand—on her shoulder and waited to see what she would do or say. Nothing.

"Aunt Hesty," I said again, and come around to face her, kneeling down on the ground in front of her. She looked at me then, her eyes were terrible.

"They sent me away," she said.

"I know." I felt my voice sicken from the knowing it. "I know they did."

"They could have kept me," Aunt Hesty said, "and told everybody we'd married before Robert left. Daddy was a judge, he could have married us even if it wasn't in the church, people would have believed it." Her face was turned away, looking down at the rock. I had the feeling I had before, when she first told me the story out at the creek, that it was the girl she was that was talking to me.

"A girl wants her mother," she said.

Her hands were holding tight onto each other in her lap. I put my fingers in between hers, worked her hands apart and took each one of them in one of mine.

"Yes," I said. "We do."

"There is all kinds of mothers," I said. I didn't know where my words was coming from, maybe from out of the mouth of the cave. "Sometimes we have to go looking for them."

She didn't answer. Pearl squatted down beside us then.

"I never found one," Aunt Hesty said. "Here I am out here having a baby of my own and no mother, not even no womenfolk to help me." She wrapped her arms around her belly and rocked. I never seen no one—not even Robbie standing out in the yard that day he first come to our house—look so much alone.

"You didn't find her, you made her, Mommy."

Now Pearl put her hands on each side of Aunt Hesty's face and turned it so that she was looking at her. "You made her out of your ownself, and out of me, out of Linney when she come, and the boys."

Seemed like Pearl's hands on her face had brought Aunt Hesty back around. Pearl nudged her shoulder just a little nudge, like a joke was coming on.

"What are you thinking now, Mommy?" she asked.

"I'm thinking that's a hell of a deal," she said to Pearl.

"I know, Mommy," Pearl said, "but it's got us this far."

I had set back on my heels while they had those words, and Pearl kept her eyes on Aunt Hesty but she reached over and pulled me back in. We sat in a little circle, our arms laced around each other's shoulders, till Aunt Hesty begun to shift her weight around how she does when she's fixing to get up.

Aunt Hesty said, "Give me a minute," and she went back into the cave.

I looked at Pearl. "You did just right," she said. Then, "This is how it was on my wedding day, only I didn't know the story till then, that was when she told me. I think it's the wedding set her off." She looked off into the trees, down the way we'd come. It was quiet. It looked to be lightening up a little overhead. Aunt Hesty come out and we walked almost the whole way home without needing to say a word.

When we got close to where we'd be coming back out of the woods, though, Aunt Hesty stopped, and squared off from Pearl and me.

"Enough already," she said. "What's it going to be?"

"What—"

"Robbie," Aunt Hesty said, looking at Pearl. Then she looked at me. "And Linney."

"Robbie will finish out what needs finished, and that'll be the end of that," Pearl said.

They both looked down at the ground then. I didn't know what that meant.

I was still carrying around that one question and I wasn't ready to ask it. But I knew enough to know that ready wasn't for what. I waited till Pearl looked up at me.

"Why?" I didn't even feel real, to be saying it out loud, "Why did you do it? Why didn't you stop it? How could you send him away?"

It seemed wrong to watch her face, but I had to know. She looked first to Aunt Hesty, who shrugged her back onto herself, then up at the sky, and back down at the ground. She wiped down her face with her hands, covered her eyes, then uncovered them, covered her mouth, and looked at me.

"I don't know," she said.

"Now, I believe that," Aunt Hesty said, but Pearl wasn't done.

"Well, I believed Virgil," she said. "He come to me, and he said there's things boys need to learn when they get to be Robbie's age. Tom and Danny, they figured them out with Virgil, but Robbie was different, he said. Close to me in a way the other boys weren't, and he needed something different. He said he couldn't explain it to me in any way that was going to make it make sense to me, nor make it any easier. Virgil is not a man that goes around trying to get his own way about every little thing, so when he told me that it was so, I believed him."

Aunt Hesty was looking a little less sure about things. "Well, Pearl," she said, "I wish you'd told me that in the beginning."

"He looks different," Pearl said, "don't you think? Like there's more of him, and I'm not talking about his arms and his back and how tall he's got."

It was true. It was a mystery, how we both of us had turned into our ownselves—such a far way from when we were sitting together out in back of the house and throwing rocks at the coal bank. How we'd got so much closer to who we really were. All kinds of borning and all kinds of dying.

"And Linney?" Aunt Hesty asked again.

Pearl and her were both looking at me with their eyebrows raised and shaking their heads yes before I even spoke. But I had to say it out loud, it had to be me that said it.

I couldn't feel my body. I thought I might be floating, that's how much I had to let go of everything to be able to ask.

I looked a long minute at both of them and still I felt like anything could happen, like I didn't know what they would say.

"Will you have me?" I said. And it was done.

We went laughing and crying the rest of the way to the edge of the woods. We hurried then, but we stopped to gather ourselves before we stepped out. I heard something snap and I thought it must be one of the boys, they'd still be out looking. But it wasn't. It was a doe and a half-grown fawn a few feet down from us, fixing to go back in just as we was coming out. Aunt Hesty caught her breath.

"Perfect," she said.

We made it to the Marcus place well before noontime. Virgil and the boys was out on the back porch, watching the tree line when we come through. They had searched all around the farm and down by the creek and had been to the house, Virgil said, about half an hour.

"I figured you to be back together pretty soon," he said, which made me think the kind of running off that Robbie had told me about had ended up this way before. "So we loaded up the wagons, except for the cakes and pies. Danny's in the house now, bundling up his clothes."

Pearl bent in at the middle just a little bit and put her hands down on her knees like somebody out of breath when Virgil said that, but me and Aunt Hesty was still standing on either side of her and we sidled in on her till she straightened back up.

"Well, now," she said. She looked past Virgil over to the window of the back room where Danny and Doug slept, then back at Virgil. "I'd not thought about that."

Danny come through the back door just then and saw we was back. "Come and see," he said, to all of us but mostly to me. We had two wagons to make the trip in, the one that Robbie had come up in made an extra for us. That's the one Danny was headed for, we seen it already had something big, with an old blanket wrapped around it, loaded up in the back. Danny pushed his bundle into the back of the wagon then climbed up and lifted the blanket for us to see.

It was a blanket chest, a nice big one, as pretty a thing as I ever seen. I climbed up in the back of the wagon too, just to put my hands on it. He'd rubbed it so smooth it almost glowed, a warm, reddish brown. There was a branch of dogwood in flower carved into the front panel, stretching out from the top right corner and reaching in a twisty, curvy way all the way over to the bottom of the other side. He'd put a little extra stain on the blossoms, so they stood out a little richer than the rest, and he'd carved a couple of small leaves on twigs over onto the top and side panels, so that it looked like the branch curved around. The corners of the lid was cut into a curve. He slid his hand over it.

"No sharp edges," he said. "I don't know how many times I knocked my head into Mamaw's chest when I was little."

Pearl looked over to Virgil and smiled. "Well, now," she said. "Imagine that."

Danny lifted the lid. He'd carved his and Delsie's names inside it and stained the writing. Delsie Marcus and Danny Chandler, September 20, 1910. There was a tiny version of the dogwood branch under their names and date. He looked at me, "Remember what you told me?" he asked. "I do," I said. "It's beautiful." And it was. He put the lid down and covered the chest back up.

"Can we go now? Are we all ready?" he asked Pearl and Virgil. He was all lit up, I never seen anything like it. I was all lit up myself, it was almost too much.

The boys had figured out that they wanted to ride together, and they all piled into the wagon with the chest. Tom drove and Walt sat on the seat beside him. Danny and Doug and Robbie fit themselves in around the chest as best they could. The boys started up the road first, there was a lot of loud talking trailing out behind them. It was quieter in our wagon. Virgil and Pearl was sitting up front and me and Aunt Hesty was in the back, bracing ourselves against the crates of canned goods to keep them from sliding, with our hands ready to grab cakes and pies when we hit a bump or Virgil called back to us to hold on. I was looking around at the trees, seeing what was starting to turn. Everything looked beautiful to me.

Aunt Hesty had been quiet. I figured she must be pretty used up from the kind of morning she'd had. "How are you holding up?" I asked her when we hit a long, straight stretch of road that meant we were almost there.

"Good enough," she said. "You know what you're going to tell them?"

I knew what she meant. "Not exactly," I said.

They wouldn't like it, Mama and Daddy. They'd almost for sure tell me I had to come home, they had no idea how far gone from them I was.

I was way past thinking I had to do what they said. That wasn't a mean feeling, though I could still feel mad about some things, it was just how much I'd changed. I was their daughter, and hoped I'd find my way back to loving them, but I would not go back to living the way they had set things up. I was not going to worry my whole life I might waste a bit of daylight, nor close my eyes and take whatever kind of life got handed to me. I would make my own.

I reached out and put my hand on the wedding quilt. It was bundled up inside an old worn out quilt to keep it clean in the wagon, but I knew what it looked like inside. I knew it had my name on it, we'd all of us signed it in tiny stitches in a corner of the back. Aunt Hesty was still looking at me, waiting for me to answer.

"I'll have my doll in my pocket," I said. "She'll know what to say."

Aunt Hesty lifted her chin up and kept her eyes on me. "She will, Linney. She surely will."

It was a busy mess when we got to the Marcus place. We was still in plenty of time to help, but there was other wagons already there too, neighbors come to help cook and set up and watch it all happen. The boys had gone quiet on the last leg of the road, but when they come in through the gate Danny was too happy to sit still a minute more. He stood up in the back of the wagon, flung both his arms up in the air like somebody that just won a big race, and started dancing some kind of jig. The wagon hit a bump though and knocked him down on his backside which set the rest of the boys off laughing even more. People was coming out onto the porch to see what was going on and started clapping and cheering when they seen all the boys picking Danny up and carrying him up to the house—Tom and Doug made a seat out of their hands and Robbie and Walt was each holding one of his feet under their arms. Then they all got too laughing so much, they couldn't hold onto him and dropped him in the yard.

"Delsie," Danny was calling toward the house, still on his hands and knees in the all-fall-down mess of brothers on the ground, but it was Mrs. Marcus come out of the back door. She was laughing too and shaking her finger at him.

"No, No, No, No, No, Danny," she said. "You don't see the bride today till you're standing before the preacher."

"You're fooling with me," he said, but she was not. "What am I supposed to do?"

"Oh, we'll think of something," Tom said. Danny didn't look too sure, but the boys all got up on their feet and dusted off, pushing on each other and still laughing every time they caught each other's eye. They pushed Danny back toward the wagon and stood around for a minute or two, figuring where to start. They come over together to where we was still standing at our wagon.

"Let's unload what stays here," Robbie said to Virgil, "then we'll take one of the wagons over to Danny and Delsie's and set their stuff up over there."

It wasn't much to carry into the house, the cakes and pies we'd baked, and all our good clothes we'd brought to change into once all the setting up was done. The boys moved the crates of canned goods over

to the wagon that had the blanket chest in it, but we
held onto the quilt. We couldn't help it, me and Pearl
and Aunt Hesty. We knew it would be nice for Delsie
to find it in her house, but we wanted to show it to her
ourselves and see how she liked it. Pearl knew which
patches had come from Danny's shirts, back to when
he was a little boy, and she needed to tell about all that.

First we got everything carried into the kitchen. I
didn't know any of the ladies in there, but there was
three or four of them come to see to the food. Pearl
seemed to know all of them pretty well, she introduced
me to them. "Our Linney," she said, and it felt even
sweeter than the first time I'd heard her say it. The ladies
shooed us out of the kitchen, though. I seen ham and
chickens, there was two or three big pots of something
on the stove and greased pans sitting out on the table
for bread or biscuits and big tubs of peeled potatoes.
We hadn't hardly had breakfast, we'd been on the road
at dinnertime and supper seemed like it was a long time
away.

I nudged Pearl with my elbow, and nodded over
toward a plate that looked like breakfast leftovers
covered over with a cloth. "Alice," she said to one of
the ladies who was Mrs. Beecham, Ted's mama, "we're
starving." She peeked under the cloth, it was a plate
of sausage biscuits. "You think anybody will care if we
take off with this?"

"Lord, no," Mrs. Beecham said. "Take it on back
with you, Delsie and Kate and the girls is in the back
room. Delsie didn't hardly eat this morning, I bet she
can use something too. There's a little pitcher of sweet
tea over there on the table if you want."

I carried the quilt and between them Pearl and
Aunt Hesty gathered up the plate and pitcher and a few

glasses from off the shelf. We knocked on the door of the back room.

"Danny, now, I told you," Mrs. Marcus said through the door, and we could hear the little girls giggling in there.

"It's us, Kate," Pearl said.

The door opened just wide enough for us to squeeze in. Delsie was sitting on the edge of the bed, with Mrs. Marcus up on the bed behind her on her knees, combing out Delsie's hair. It was wet. Delsie had a little slip on and a towel around her shoulders. The whole room smelled of some sweet kind of soap. Even wet, her hair was curly as could be. Mrs. Marcus was taking a little handful at a time and working her way up from the bottom with the comb. It was going to take a while. Delsie started to get up when we come in, but she got held back by the comb stuck in her hair.

"We'll come to you, honey," Pearl said. She set down the plate on the chest of drawers and went over to hold Delsie's face in her hands. "Sweetheart," she said, and kissed Delsie's face. Her and Mrs. Marcum looked at each other the way they did that day on the porch.

"Pearl, now, don't get me started," Mrs. Marcus said.

"No, no," Pearl said. "I know."

Then everybody hugged everybody all the way around and we got out the sausage biscuits and tea. "Where is Danny?" Delsie asked.

"Over to your house," I told her. And that felt so surprising to say, I said it again, "Your house." A little shiver blew across her shoulders. Her mama asked her was she cold, she said no.

Mrs. Marcus was still combing, but her and Pearl and Aunt Hesty was talking together, so me and Delsie begun to talk around them.

"He's brought you something," I said, "and they've took it on over there. Did you hear them out front?"

"Just a little," she said. "Does he look scared?"

"Not one bit, just quiet every once in a while, looking at Pearl and Virgil and all the rest of them. I never seen anybody so shiny," I told her. "He's about coming out of his skin, that's how happy he is." I wanted to ask her if she was scared, but not while everybody else was around.

Mrs. Marcus had finally got done with the comb and they had come around to talking about the quilt, so we all got up to hold it out and look at it. Pearl told all she wanted to tell and we flipped the corner over to see where we'd all signed it. "Turns out I can quilt almost as fast as Pearl," I said, and Aunt Hesty told them how they couldn't get me away from it once I got started.

"I love everything about it," Delsie said, and she hugged it up to her chest. "I love my life." She looked over at her mama, and there was no help for the tears then. You wouldn't even want there to be.

It went so fast after that. When it was time for Delsie to get dressed, she stood in the middle of the room in her slip and we all stood around her. Mrs. Marcus had Katie sweep around the floor one more time just to be sure, then between us all we lowered the dress onto her upraised arms and dropped it down. It wasn't a big fancy dress, just bleached muslin, but done up so sweet, with a plain cut bodice, covered with twining vines and leaves and bell-shaped blossoms embroidered in white thread, that cinched in under her bosom in tiny tucks. The sleeves was gathered just a little at the top, but flared loose between her wrists and elbows, with a little vine embroidered there too. The skirt looked like it was cut from a circle, with waves of vines and blossoms reaching up from the hem. I couldn't believe how much the flowers and vines looked like what Danny had carved into the blanket chest.

There was a moment when I seen all our arms up and reaching toward her, her arms held up too, for the dress to slide on—Delsie's so graceful and round, Pearl's and Mrs. Marcus's showing all their years of work, Aunt Hesty's twisted looking as a grapevine, mine mismatched but both held up, and the little girl's arms barely holding on. I seen in my head the way the tree limbs arched over the creek that morning out on the rock while Aunt Hesty told me her story. I seen how different this story was from hers, how Danny and Delsie were making their own story. All of it felt like church.

The ladies went off to another room to get dressed and Delsie stayed with me while I got my dress on. I stepped out of my work dress, I hadn't known what a mess it was from our going out after Aunt Hesty that morning till I seen it laying on the floor. I walked across the room for the little wash pitcher Mrs. Marcus had put out for me while Delsie stood still by the bed, not sitting down so as not to wrinkle her dress.

"I'm getting married," she said. "Today."

"I know."

"Today," she said again.

"Well, now," I said. "I can see how—" I didn't know what word to use. There was only one that felt true, but it was so strange to say. "I can see how a woman might be kind of scared about some things. I don't really know about that, Delsie. But I know about Danny."

She didn't say nothing.

"You do too," I said.

"I do know," Delsie said after a long moment of watching her hands holding onto each other. She looked down at her dress like she was surprised to find out it was real. "Alright."

I was into my own dress then. "You'll have to button me up," I said, for it was done up snug in the waist and I couldn't quite twist around to do it myself. I stood with my back to her, facing the long mirror and she did me up. I felt her hands on my shoulders and she put her face next to mine from behind.

"Beautiful," she said. "Remember?"

We was holding up our skirts so we could see to step into our shoes when Pearl and Mrs. Marcus and Aunt Hesty come back knocking on the door.

"Ready?" Mrs. Marcus asked, and we both of us answered "Yes."

The house was empty as we walked through, just Mr. Marcus waiting inside the back door. We could see through the screen door that everybody was gathered out in the yard, around the shade trees. Danny and the preacher was standing there, and all the boys and Virgil right around. Neighbors and people from their church and some of the Marcus cousins and their families was standing off a little ways, visiting and waiting. Somebody caught sight of us standing inside the door and everybody turned toward the house and got quiet. We all walked out except Delsie and her daddy, and we stood up by the preacher with Danny. Then they come out and Danny and Delsie was standing up there in front of the preacher.

I couldn't say what all was said, a lot of it was Bible talk. At some point, though, the preacher said, "Join hands," and I took Aunt Hesty's. I realized after a minute he was only talking to Danny and Delsie, but that didn't matter. When Danny pulled that little ring out of his pocket, the one Aunt Hesty's mother had give her to pretend she was married with when she come to Kentucky, her whole body clenched up so hard I thought she might leave bruises on my hand.

I thought it must be the wedding she never got that was hurting her, but when I looked over she didn't look hurt, she looked like somebody who just won. She was staring at Danny and Delsie, like everybody else. "Good boy," she said, real quiet. She seen me looking at her. "Finally," she whispered, "it's a real wedding ring."

When the preacher started in with the "Do you" questions there was something about that I took for my own. It wasn't the exact promises that felt meant for me, it was the promising itself.

I would keep with Pearl and all of them, and they would keep with me. I would say out loud things I needed to say and ask out loud what I needed to ask. I wouldn't let anything false come into it, not toward them, not toward me. Not from the outside, and not from the inside. I promised myself and all of them, I would be true. I would be true.

Then it was over, Danny was kissing Delsie and swinging her around and there was all kinds of whooping and hollering and everybody pushing up to where they was to get in on all that happiness. Some of the ladies took off toward the house, though, and started bringing out loads of food from the kitchen and laying it out on tables they must have set up on the back porch while we was all inside getting ready. It was too crowded up there around Danny and Delsie so I went into the kitchen and carried whatever they told me to pick up out to wherever they told me to put it. Robbie come in looking for me just as we was getting the last of it out. I hadn't hardly seen him, what with Aunt Hesty and the wedding and all. The ladies had him holler at everybody to come and eat. There was more tables set up in the yard, and some picnic blankets around.

"How about that red blanket over by the side of the house?" I said to him. "Let's get our plates and go over there where it's not so loud."

I was so hungry, I tried to take some of everything, but I run out of room on my plate before I even got to the second food table on the porch—ham and chicken, it had been dumplings in one of them big pots on the stove, corn, mashed potatoes, cabbage slaw, cucumbers and tomatoes. I got over to the blanket before Robbie, when he come he was holding his plate underneath with one hand and holding his other hand spread out overtop to keep his pile of supper from falling off. We didn't talk much at first, just ate and looked around, pointing at people eating and laughing and acting sweet. Finally, no more food would fit and I leaned back against the side of the house. Robbie was leaned over his plate in his lap still, but he was slowing way down. I could see Virgil and Pearl from where we was, they was standing with Aunt Hesty over by one of the tables in the yard where Danny and Delsie was sitting. Danny was eating one-handed, he was keeping his other hand on top of Delsie's on the table between their plates.

"Robbie," I said. He turned his face to me, a forkful of mashed potatoes was still on its way up to his face. "I'm staying." He stared at me, that fork slid out of his hand and turned its little pile of mashed potatoes over onto the blanket. He watched me pick up the little pile of potato and throw it over into the grass.

"Do they know?" he asked, when I had brushed off my hand with the edge of the blanket and looked over to him again.

"I told Pearl and Aunt Hesty this morning that I wanted to stay," I told him, "so I expect Virgil knows by now." Virgil had hugged me so hard when we were getting in the wagon to come, and said what he always said, to let him know if I needed anything. Anything at all, he said. I knew what he meant. "The rest of them don't know yet, I'm not thinking we'll tell them till we get home, but I couldn't not tell you."

I could feel my face starting to grin. His was too.

"Wait," he said. "Will they let you?"

It was Mama and Daddy he meant.

"It's not theirs to say. I'm grown," I said, and I knew I was.

"Yes," Robbie said. He looked out at the yard for a minute. "We didn't die of it," he said.

"We didn't. We're right here."

"Oh," he said, "Linney, I can't wait to be home for good."

He started grinning again and tossed a biscuit up in the air and caught it. He tossed another one and then he was on his knees on the blanket juggling biscuits. I couldn't believe what I was seeing.

I seen Pearl start laughing and nudge Aunt Hesty and Virgil and point over to where we was. Other people started watching then and laughing. When Robbie caught sight that he was being watched, he caught one biscuit in his mouth and set it aside real quick with his hand, till they was all gone. It was silly, but Pearl was right, there was more to him now. He took a little bow from his waist and everybody clapped and went on with what they was doing. He sat back down, both of us leaning against the house and looking out. He didn't look at me, but he patted my hand, then with his same hand patted over his heart.

"Nothing removed about us," he said.

The light was beginning to change, for it was September after all and well after suppertime. It was a bit of a chill coming on too. There was some men working on starting a fire, we could hear them talking over each other as to how much wood to start with, how to set the pile, what to start it with. There was the sound of dishes being piled up and carried in, but the ladies in the kitchen had told us all we was not to lift a finger in the cleaning up and that was alright with me because I didn't want to be anywhere else but where I was. Here and there somebody would laugh or holler out something loud, but under that was a softer sound of people talking, and under that a softer sound of crickets and the wind starting shuffle the high-up leaves. I leaned my head over on Robbie's shoulder thinking I'd rest my eyes just for minute, but then there was some scratchy fiddle sounds coming from the porch, and some guitar notes and little sprinkles of a mandolin and banjo. I could feel Robbie sitting up straighter and looking around to see what was going on.

"I seen Mr. Hartsell was here," he said. "He calls dances better than anybody around."

He started pulling me up to my feet, but I was feeling how long a day it had been. There was no help for it though. Here come the rest of them to pull us into the middle. All of us and all the Marcuses was in a big circle holding hands, everybody else was holding hands in an even bigger circle around us. I was between Robbie and Aunt Hesty.

"I don't know how," I told them. "Really."

"You don't have to know how," Robbie said.

"Just follow," Aunt Hesty said.

A waltz started coming out from the porch, a little bit quiet, and steady, the way the waves in a river will be steady even though they're all different. Mr. Hartsell said a few things to start out. The inner circle, he said, circles to the left, and the outer circle to the right. Get yourselves so it's Lady-Gent-Lady-Gent. When the ladies are handing off, the gentlemen are not moving. And if you get lost, just jump back in wherever you are and hold on. Then he said One-Two-Three and it begun.

First we circled till the music got in us and even though I was just walking it felt like dancing. Ladies turned right then, and took whoever was there to be our partner. I was with Robbie still and he told me so easy how to step one-two-three, my underneath hand set so easy around his waist and my other hand on his shoulder. We waltzed in place there till Mr. Hartsell called "Ladies hand off." Robbie took my hand down from his shoulder and swung me a slow swing toward the center till I was facing the next gentleman, which was Mr. Marcus. He was holding his hand out to catch mine and he swung me a slow curve toward the outside of the circle then handed me off to the next gentleman waiting in the circle. All the ladies was weaving in and out that way till we come back to our first partners.

It was the most beautiful feeling, to be so graceful, to feel how the graceful of it was rising up out of what we was all doing together. Then we turned right again

and there was a new partner. We went on and on
till we come back around to our first partners. "Last
time around," Mr. Hartsell called, and when that
was over, "Bow to your partner and say good-night."
He looked over to where Danny and Delsie was
standing, then at Virgil and Pearl, and Mr. and Mrs.
Marcus. The four of them all nodded to him and so
then Mr. Hartsell called out to everyone again, "And
give the bride and groom a cheer and wish them a
good night."

Everybody started hollering and carrying on
and Delsie hid her face in Danny's shirt. The boys
all gathered around them and lifted them onto the
Marcus's wagon and slapped the horse on the rump
and they went off to their house. We all didn't know
quite what to do after that, seemed like it happened
so all of a sudden. The music kept coming though
and people started to square up for other kinds of
dances. "I don't know," I told Robbie. "I think I want
to hold on to that dance a little while before I try
another one. Let's get a drink and rest a minute."
Aunt Hesty was back beside us, "Come on, Mamaw,"
Robbie said. "We'll get you a drink and sit a minute."

We got some jars of tea and went around to the
front porch, away from the party. There was a lamp
on in the front room, it give a little yellow light out
onto the porchboards, enough to see by. Me and Aunt
Hesty sat on the porch swing and Robbie sat on the
floor, all the extra chairs had been carried around
back. I nudged the square of yellow light with my toe
and set the porch swing to moving.

"Lord, Linney, don't do that," Aunt Hesty said.
"If you rock me I'll nod off right now and you and
Robbie'll have to carry me to bed."

I was thinking it was a good thing we was staying the night, or else I might need carried too. And maybe that's what happened, because thinking that thought and laying my head on Aunt Hesty's shoulder is the very last thing I remember about that day.

After and Before

September 1910

I WOKE UP NEXT MORNING in Delsie's old bed, already thinking about going home. It put a little shiver of excitement through my heart, for I would be crossing a threshold too. To a house that was mine in a way that it wasn't, exactly, before. I didn't hear any noises from the Marcus's kitchen, so I pulled the covers up over my shoulder and turned on my side toward the window. I was thinking about my first day waking up at Chandlers' and walking into the kitchen not knowing what to call Pearl.

I knew there wasn't a word, exactly, for them to call me, now that I was there to stay. "Sister" would work for the boys. Except for Robbie. Something the same had happened to us that made us know each other differently, like sharing a secret, even though there was nothing hid about it. Virgil and Pearl, they weren't Mama and Daddy to me, I was all but grown by the time I got to them.

And whatever it was between me and Aunt Hesty, all the things she told and taught me—I had a feeling like that was something very old, very deep, going on way back before us, maybe since the beginning of the world.

I'd just be Linney in my new family—there was no other name for it. Already I'd heard Virgil and Pearl talking about "our Linney" to people at the wedding. That was fine by me.

"I couldn't hurry to save my life," Pearl was saying to Mrs. Marcus when I finally got myself out of bed and into the kitchen.

"Nor cook neither," Mrs. Marcus said, and I seen they'd laid out in the kitchen all kinds of food left over from the wedding party for breakfast. "Anybody wants eggs'll have to go out and snatch them out from under the chickens theirself."

Pearl put me a cup of coffee on the table and the three of us sat there not saying much of anything, then Aunt Hesty come in and sat beside me, across from Pearl. The rest of them started coming in soon enough, everybody dragging a little. The boys ended up at one end of the table, looking at each other over their plates like something was off and they couldn't quite get their heads around it.

There wasn't no getting around it. They made a different shape and everything they said sounded different with Danny not there. Robbie, too, was still a little quiet around them. But Mrs. Marcus kept pouring coffee and we all got some food and some feeling back in us.

"Well, now," Aunt Hesty said. "Well, now," and then she picked up her coffee cup and leaned back in her chair like she expected an answer.

"What, Mommy?" Pearl asked her.

"That's what I'm saying, Pearl. Now what? What?"

"That's a pretty big question, Mommy," Pearl said. "What makes you think I know?" Then she leaned over the table toward Aunt Hesty and started singing under her breath, "Jesus loves me, He don't know..." which made me laugh and snort and spew about half a cup of coffee all across the table, then everybody was laughing without knowing quite why, the way you do when you been working so hard and holding things inside for too long and finally, on the other side of whatever it is, it all lets go—laughing or crying or all of it mixed up together.

Once we'd mostly got a hold of ourselves, Virgil and the boys started talking amongst themselves down at their end of the table, so we come out into the front room to sit with the rest of our coffee till we could see— at least for that day—what was coming next. I think that's what they was talking about in the kitchen too. First I heard something about bedrooms now Danny was out of the house, then somehow it was talk about acreage and fields.

Seemed like Pearl was keeping half an ear on what was going on in there, but when she seen Ollie brushing crumbs off the seat of the rocker before she sat down, she started looking around her.

The front room looked like every single thing in it had been picked up and shook around and left anywhere but where it belonged. Even though the neighbor women had cleaned up a lot, there was still a mess of dishes and pots and food all over the kitchen, and you could see where people had come in to sit and eat all over the house. Not to mention all the getting ready we'd done getting into our wedding clothes in the bedrooms.

"We are not leaving Kate with this mess," Pearl said.

"We need some fairies or some elves," I said. "Like them that come in the night and clean everything up or make the shoes or spin the straw."

"Well, what we got is us," Pearl said. "Sooner we get started, sooner we'll get done."

That suited me. I was getting pictures in my head of Chandlers' front porch—our front porch, I'd have to get used to saying things that way—and Pearl standing at the worktable in the kitchen, and Robbie coming home to stay soon as he could.

Pearl and Mrs. Marcus told the little girls to start in the front room, wiping down and sweeping up. The two of them would take on the kitchen and me and Aunt Hesty was to start in the bedrooms, just making the beds and tidying what we could see to tidy. Pearl tugged at my sleeve a bit and told me in my ear to keep a good eye on her, tired as she was, she was more like to go off. She turned toward the kitchen, then back toward me.

"You've give her a lot," Pearl said, "whether you know it or not." She put a hand on either side of my face and her eyes held mine for a second. Then she let go with both hands, like you'd let go a little bird you was giving back to the air. "Off to it, then, Linney!" she called back over her shoulder. She was happy, Pearl was.

So was I, though it was strange being in Delsie's room without it being her room anymore. Me and Aunt Hesty made the bed together, one of us on either side, how you do, tossing and smoothing and patting.

"You'll be needing a new quilt next," she said.

"I don't think so!" I thought she was talking about me getting married next and I wasn't looking for that. I had a whole family I'd just got.

She got herself settled down on the bed, her back propped up with pillows and her legs straight out in front of her. It was a pretty bed, wood painted white, the headboard cut with a curve across the top and a rounded edge Mr. Marcus must have smoothed down by hand. I was casting my eyes around the room, seeing what there was to pick up. A few things were mine, I put them in a pile just outside the door. There was some pallets made up on the floor, for little ones that had to be brought in to sleep when the supper and the dancing went late. I'd start there, fold the quilts and blankets, and set them at the foot of the bed.

"Listen when I'm talking to you, Linney," Aunt Hesty said, loud enough to bring Katie to the bedroom door. I waved Katie off.

I went and sat on the very edge of Delsie's bed, Aunt Hesty not scooting over one bit to make room for me. Without looking back at her, I reached my arm behind me and put my hand on her shoulder.

"I'm in a hurry to get home, I guess," I said. "It's something about this room, makes me want to be in my own." I shifted on the bed to where I could see her face. "It'll be the first time I know it's all the way mine." I took an extra breath. "That is not nothing."

"Well, what did you think I was talking about, Linney? We got a quilt to make for your room. Best be thinking about how you want it."

So we talked about that, and new curtains and rag rugs, and when I picked up a quilt to fold we looked at it good before I put it in a pile with the others. Turned out I liked a lot of little pieces, and a lot of colors, but a lot of white too, so you could do something a little bit fancy in the plain spaces. There was a postage stamp quilt made with lots of little squares stitched up together, spaced with big white squares so that they went criss-cross on the quilt that I liked.

"I don't know, though, how that would look with the kinds of pieces we've got," I said. "All them boy shirts, won't they just all blend together? And would they even look right set with white?" I looked at Delsie's bed and I couldn't picture a quilt made up like that on it.

"We'll see what Kate's got," Aunt Hesty said. "All these girls here, there's bound to be a lot and we could use up all the littlest pieces that won't do for much else. And me and Pearl's saved back all the scraps from our things. There's a good bit, we've not had much call to use it up. We've got the scraps from the dress we made you for the wedding. Anyway, it's a quilt, Linney. There's no knowing what it's gonna look like till it's all done. It'll keep us busy though and give us some color to look at through the winter."

"I wish we was home now." I let my shoulders sag. "I think all that coffee's wearing off."

"I expect we've got to clean up after this business before we can move onto the next, so keep folding and stacking, and we'll be pulling up into the yard before we know it. We'll all of us need a good long rest."

"I hope so," I said. "What do you think Virgil and the boys was talking about?" I'd been trying to listen in too, to hear what Robbie was saying because we'd only had that little bit of time at the wedding supper since he got home. But Ollie was telling some big story about a witchy house somewhere out in the woods.

"The boys are thinking about going home too, I reckon," Aunt Hesty said. "Now Danny's got his place in the world figured out, I expect the others are wondering how they're gonna end up. Seems pretty clear Tom's the one will run things around the place when Virgil's ready for somebody to take over. That leaves Doug and Robbie and Walt. I just don't know how many little families that place can feed. It's a lot to think about. Nothing like a wedding to get a person thinking about what's waiting around the bend."

Not me, I thought, but I didn't say it out loud. I was ready to go home and for nothing to happen except that quilt and Robbie coming home to stay. I wanted things to settle and stay settled long as ever they could. I wanted to know Robbie wasn't thinking about going off anywhere else once he got home.

We got the house back in order by dinnertime and Virgil and Mr. Marcus and the boys had got the horses ready and the wagons straightened up, and brought them around to the front of the house to load up. There wasn't near as much to load and carry for the trip back home. Pearl and Virgil was a little too quiet, standing together in front of the two wagons empty of Danny and all his things, and Delsie's chest, and all the canned goods we'd packed in along with food for the wedding. The rest of us had gathered ourselves up in the front room with whatever else we'd brought ourselves all packed up. Lots of things were going to feel a whole lot more real once we got on the road and the wedding was behind us.

Seemed like it took forever for everybody to hug everybody else and say whatever they had left to say. Finally Virgil clapped his hands real big.

"Alright now," he said. "We all know everybody loves everybody, but if some of us don't get on the road we'll be getting home in the dark." He started herding us all toward the porch. "And I don't want to see nobody stopping on the porch, straight on into the wagons, now."

We all did stop on the porch though, for here come two men on horseback riding in just fast enough that we all stopped on the porch to watch them come. One was a man I remembered seeing at the wedding. The other one I'd never seen before.

The stranger was a preacher, come up by way of Pike County. It had been raining down there pretty hard for some days. The Tug was high, he said, and it wasn't only that. It was running fast enough that it was carving out big chunks of the riverbank from underneath, felling trees that was damming it up here and there. People that had highwater houses was carrying their canned goods and quilts and whatever mattered to them most up to them little hilltop shacks people who lived right on the river oftentimes built on their land. You could sleep up there too, if it come night and you didn't know what was going to happen.

Daddy never would build one. He said it was like courting a flood to make a place like that. Waste of time, he said. Better to build an extra chicken coop, cut more brush, make fence posts—make more.

We all just stared at that preacher till he looked away, like he was studying something up along the ridgeline. Somebody put their hand on my back, and I was glad we was all standing in a bunch like that on the porch. Virgil spoke to him.

"Any word about folks down on the river?" he asked. "You hear anything about Carl Stepp and his family?"

"I've told you all I know, " he said. "But I was awful glad to be coming up this way, I can tell you that."

"Well come on in then," Mrs. Marcus told him. "We've had a wedding so there's plenty of food, even if it's not a proper dinner."

And we all of us went back in.

Once the preacher and his friend had gone on their way, we found ourselves all gathered together back in the front room. I don't even know how to say what it felt like. Like a flood, maybe, like the Tug had got inside me and pushed everything around. Except for one thing. I still knew I was where I belonged— with Virgil and Pearl, and Aunt Hesty and the boys, wherever they were.

But I wouldn't be able to figure out what that meant for the old home I was leaving until I'd told them there what I decided. I was trying to picture all the rooms in that house, what they looked like when I left, when Virgil clapped his hands real big again.

"We'll go first light," he said. "It's got too late in the day to try now. We couldn't hardly get down there before dark in good weather and we've got to at least be able to see what's in front of us if we know we're like to meet trouble."

He said something about stopping by home first, for buckets and mops and brooms. Virgil said they'd figure out what tools they might need in the morning.

"We don't even know," Virgil seemed to be talking to me. "Likely we'll get down there and there won't be no more trouble than a lot of mud. Maybe not even all the way up into the house. We'll get down there fast as we can."

That was when I understood what the rest of them was thinking. That part hadn't gone into my head straight away, that people can die in floods. All I could feel was so, so tired, and I wanted so bad to get home to the room that was truly mine, now.

They figured some more. We'd all go except for Pearl and Aunt Hesty and Walt. It wouldn't be safe, taking Aunt Hesty down there and none of us knowing what we would be up against. Pearl and Walt could carry on at home between them. We'd all be back home before we knew it, Virgil said.

"What about Danny?" Robbie asked.

"Absolutely not," Pearl said at the same Aunt Hesty and I said "No."

"Kate, let's you and me go see what kind of food we've got that'll travel and last," Pearl said. "And gather up whatever we can for cleaning."

That's what they did, and Virgil and Mr. Marcus and the boys went out to the barn to gather up anything out there they thought might be useful. That left me and Aunt Hesty, and Katie and Ollie in the front room not knowing what to do with ourselves. Aunt Hesty hollered toward the kitchen for Mrs. Marcus to come back a minute.

"Me and Linney got a plan for making a quilt for her room," she said. "You think we could go through your scrap bag for some little pieces, dress goods?"

Mrs. Marcus had Katie and Ollie drag two big bushel baskets full of scraps, all colors, pieces in all kinds of shapes and sizes, out of the big bedroom.

"Take as much as you want," she told us. "We haven't even cut into this year's feedsacks, I like to save sewing for cold weather work."

I never saw so many pretty pieces all at once. I felt shy to take things, but Katie and Ollie started making a pile for me. They talked and talked while they picked through the basket, remembering what Mrs. Marcus had made for them out of this piece or that, things they did when they was wearing this dress or that, birthdays and trips to town and church dinners. I was glad for their talk, and for how those scrap baskets kept my eyes busy enough to give my head a rest. Aunt Hesty cut a couple pieces about two inches square and give one of them to each of the girls.

"Go ahead and cut some patches," she told them. "Get as many different prints and colors as you can, to start. We'll be having rows of five or six print squares, set on a slant," she was talking me now. "Let's say five. So as the girls start getting you a pile of patches to work with, start sorting them into rows like I taught you with Danny and Delsie's quilt. Katie, you know where your mommy's sewing basket is? Bring Linney a little handful of pins and she can stack the little piles of patches by row and pin them together so's they'll be all ready to pick up and sew when things calm down."

We worked on, not exactly peaceful but calm enough, till suppertime. Pearl and Mrs. Marcus had fried up some potatoes and ham to go with the leftovers. Nobody talked much. When Virgil and Mr. Marcus pushed back from the table, everybody looked to them.

"Let's get things wrapped up and get off to bed soon as we can," Virgil said. "It's been a long day and tomorrow's gonna be longer." He wiped his hand down his face, how he does when things are getting to be too much. "Anybody got anything they need to talk about? Anything we maybe didn't think of yet?"

Nobody did. The boys wandered off to the rooms they were sleeping in. The Marcus girls started in washing dishes Mrs. Marcus shooed us out of the kitchen.

"We'll take care of this," Mrs. Marcus said. "You three go sit a minute and catch your breath."

We went out onto the front porch, I sat down between them in the porch swing. Aunt Hesty told Pearl about the quilt and how we'd spent the afternoon.

"Good," Pearl said. "Good, good, good. Good to be putting things together when it feels like they're coming apart." She patted my knee. "I'm off to bed."

Me and Aunt Hesty stayed a little bit longer. "Can I sleep with you?" I asked her. Delsie's bed would hold us both. I went in and dug my nightgown out of my bundle again and got changed. I was under the covers when Aunt Hesty got in and I backed my back right up against hers so I could feel she was there. All night long I dreamed I was running alongside the river and barely keeping my footing on the bank. I had an iron pot full of red-hot coals in my hand for borrowed fire, but it was going cold fast, faster than I could run.

Almost Anything

"Linney, Linney." Katie was shaking my shoulder to wake me up. It was still all the way dark in the room. I heard her, but I couldn't pry myself awake. She shook me again and I felt Aunt Hesty turn and groan. "Cousin Virgil says best get on the way," Katie whispered. "Here's your clothes," she said, and I felt her put something in my hand.

I remembered my dream, then I remembered what was happening. I got myself propped up on my elbows, then fell back on the pillow. My head weighed about a hundred pounds. Aunt Hesty shifted again and I felt the bed lift as she got out of it. She come around to my side and tugged on my arm till I was sitting up. She unbuttoned my nightgown and set the pile of clothes Katie brought in on my lap.

"Get dressed under the covers," she said, "it's took a chill out here."

Everybody else was up and moving around when we got to the kitchen. Katie brought us both a hot cup of coffee and we sat at the table with Robbie and Walt. Pearl and Mrs. Marcus was packing up baskets of food, talking about what would keep. Mrs. Marcus kept telling Pearl to take as much as she could, because we didn't know what we'd find when we got there, it could be almost anything.

"Could you eat anything now, Linney?" Mrs. Marcus asked.

I could not. I was shaking from the cold kitchen and waking up too early. And then there was trying to figure out how to tell Mama and Daddy I wasn't coming home to stay.

"Linney needs something to wrap up in," Robbie told Katie, and she jumped up to fetch me something. She brought back a green wool knitted shawl, come up behind my chair and wrapped it around me.

"Daddy and them are out getting the wagon ready," Robbie told me and Aunt Hesty. "They're looking for a way to rig up some kind of cover for us in case we come into rain, and seeing if they've got any tools or such here that we might need."

Out the kitchen window I could see the dark was just starting to thin. The coffee and the shawl had begun to calm my shakes.

"We'll stop home before we go on down," Robbie went on, "to drop off Mama and Aunt Hesty and Walt, and pick up some more clothes and whatever else Daddy figures we need. You can sleep some more on the way down, Linney. We'll see to it you got a place to sleep in the wagon. Cousin Al's going to come down to our place after dinnertime every day till we get home and see to anything they need help with. If they do need anything." He looked at Walt, who was as serious-looking as the rest of us. "Walt will be there."

"I will," he said, and you could see it was true.

"Everybody gather up your things," Pearl said. "I see them coming out of the barn with the wagon."

I started to get up, but Katie had already got all my things together for me and brought them bundled up in an extra sweater. I told her thank you.

"I'd do anything for you, Linney," she said, and I seen that was true too.

We all went out onto the front porch and they brung the wagon right up to us. Virgil give me and Pearl and Aunt Hesty a hand into the back, then the boys all got in. The Marcus's stood out on the porch, hands raised to wave till we was out of sight. We drove past Danny and Delsie's little house, their windows was all still dark. "Good," I thought. "Good, good, good."

"We're here, Linney." This time it was Pearl waking me up in the wagon. "Get some work clothes together and some warm clothes, and then we'll all have something to eat in our own kitchen before you start back out again."

We all of us kind of fell out of the back of the wagon, and Tom took the horses off to the barn to feed them and give them a little rest. Everybody went off in different directions in the house. It was daylight by then, but dusty feeling and darkish still inside. I was in my room gathering up clothes when I heard Pearl in the kitchen making coffee and talking to Aunt Hesty. I sat on my bed for a minute and closed my eyes to hear them better. It was not the words I was listening for, but how their voices rose and caught on each other, then fell away and lifted back up, over and over. It felt as good as a warm bed and as beautiful to my ears as that wedding waltz.

I was the last one back in the kitchen. Pearl had done up a pan of scrambled eggs and brought in one of the wedding food baskets and spread it all out on the table. "Eat whatever you can," she said, "it won't last, and there's still two baskets out in the wagon. And you got work ahead of you," she added.

I ate but I couldn't have said what. And I couldn't say I was awake and thinking, but I was beginning to have pictures flash through my head. Daddy in Paintsville counting out pennies into our hands. Mama in her rocker on the porch, telling me it wasn't her fault. And some pictures that wasn't even exactly mine, like Daddy's mama clearing the table and eating what was left on the plates. I was remembering that dream I had back in the spring, where I didn't know what house I was in.

I put my hands down on the table to steady myself. Where I was in that moment, that was home. I was clear on that much.

"You alright, Linney?" Virgil said. He was still a minute, he looked like he was thinking all the way down to Pike County, to what all might waiting for us down there. I could not think that far. He looked over at Pearl. Then back at me while he rubbed up and down his jaw with his thumb and forefinger, then back to Pearl. He took his hand down. "Listen," he said. "Maybe we ought to think about whether or not Linney needs to go down there right now."

"Linney?" Pearl asked, and everybody looked at me.

It was like the laurel—there was things I had to know and things I had to say for myself, and no way around it—I had to go through. But it wouldn't do to think too much about it.

"I don't want to," I said. "But I have to, so I'm going."

"Well, we're going with you," Robbie said, and they all nodded.

Aunt Hesty pushed her chair back and walked out to the front room. I thought she was mad at me, or thought I was wrong, or I don't know what—I only knew I didn't want her walking off. She was back in a minute, carrying in the family Bible from off the mantel. I was surprised. All I'd ever heard her talk Bible-wise was about what Jesus don't know. I was not of a mind for Bible talk. It hit me how much I needed to say what I needed to say to Mama and Daddy.

"Mommy, what are you doing?" Pearl said.

Aunt Hesty set the Bible on the kitchen table and opened out a long folded page right in the front, about four times as wide as the other pages, full of hand drawn-lines and hand-written names. I leaned forward to see. The family tree. She had an ink pen in her hand. Everybody stood quiet and she moved her finger down and across, reading names. "Virgil Thomas Chandler and Pearl Lively Clark," she begun. Then she traced across the boys' names till she come to Danny's. "Daniel Lucas Chandler," she drew a little line in the space beside Danny's name and paused. "What's Delsie's given name?" she asked Pearl.

"Adelaide," Pearl said. "Adelaide Pearl Marcus."

Of course, I thought, Mrs. Marcus would have done that. Aunt Hesty wrote it in. It was almost like watching them get married again. Aunt Hesty moved her fingers along, and read out Doug's and Robbie's and Walt's given names. She left a space after Walt's, for whoever he might marry and drew another little line. She looked up at me, then everybody did. I didn't know why.

"Linney?" she said.

Then I knew. "Wait," I said.

She laid down the pen and leaned on her knuckles over the table toward me. "Whatever for?" she asked, and it was all I could do to look at her.

"It's not what you think," I said. "I should tell them first. When we get back, let's do it when we get back."

"Mommy," Pearl said, for Aunt Hesty was staring at me something awful, "Linney knows what she needs to do, now let her do it."

"Can I see it?" I asked. I wanted a picture of it in my head, with that space after Walt's, to carry with me on the trip. Aunt Hesty grunted some, but she slid the Bible over to me. I run my hand over the names. I looked to see if Robert's name was there. It was, Robert Allen Clark, just as it should have been. And beside it, Hestia Clara Lively.

"Hestia?" I never thought of it being anything but Hester.

"Goddess of home and hearth," Pearl said, "and innermost things. Judge Lively, he got one or two things right." I looked up at Aunt Hesty then and she looked back at me and a lot of what had happened between us begun to make a different kind of sense.

"I have to go." That wasn't what I meant to say to her, but it was how it came out.

"I know you do. Go on then." She picked up the Bible, carried it back out to the front room and set it back on the mantel.

Virgil told the boys to get their coats and go on out to the wagon. "You too, Linney," he said. I told him I needed a minute and went back to my room.

I pulled my box Daddy made me out from under my bed and opened it. I had to lift out everything else, the papers and pencil and the ribbons, to find the penny.

It looked small and not so shiny, but it still tasted like blood. I couldn't pretend any longer it didn't have two sides.

All the worried faces watching my face since we'd got word, I knew they'd been thinking that Mama and Daddy might be gone already. And I knew it might be so. I'd learned enough from Aunt Hesty to know you couldn't grab hold of the next thing without letting go of what had come before. I couldn't explain myself, so I hoped nobody would ask me, how I was able to imagine going on without them. Maybe I'd already been sad enough about how it was between us all along.

I looked around for something to wrap the penny in. I pulled a cloth out of the little monthly basket under my bed. I wrapped it around the penny and pinned the ends closed, running the pin as many times as I could, like as if I was quilting, through that cloth and the cloth of my apron inside the pocket. My choice was made, but I needed it with me all the same.

It was getting dark when we got there. We run into some rain and some muddy roads on the way, but nothing that the boys couldn't push the wagon out of after a little bit of trying. I couldn't tell at first just when we come in, for Daddy and Robbie had cleared so much for new fields after I left that the land itself looked different. Robbie was standing up back behind the wagon seat and holding onto the back of the seat behind Virgil to see better and tell him how to go.

"When we make the turn around that stand of trees," he told Virgil, "then we'll see the house."

I got up on my knees so I could see between Virgil's and Tom's shoulders. We come around the bend and stopped. It was all dark. There was not a lamp on in the house, though in just a few minutes it would be too dark to see even the outline of the house from where we was, at what Robbie said was the edge of the tobacco field.

"Light us a lantern," Tom said to Doug. It took a minute for Doug to feel around for the lantern and to get a match struck. He handed it to Tom, and Tom lifted it up over toward where we could hear the river running. Then he lowered it down toward the ground. "There's standing water," he said, "probably ruined the tobacco, but it don't look too bad, not dangerous bad. Can't really tell by this light, though, how high it got."

"Well, let's go on up," Virgil said. "You alright with that, Linney?"

I must have said yes, and he set the horses to head on up toward the house. We didn't get very far before the wagon wheels mired down in the mud. It felt all wrong, but also like it wasn't really happening.

I wasn't feeling the kinds of things it seemed like I was supposed to feel, the kind of things that made everybody keep looking at me and checking on me.

I started to climb out the back of the wagon. The rest of them did too. There was no sense in trying to push the wagon out if there was no dry place to push it to. Robbie pointed out the barn to Tom and he took lantern and the horses and got them settled while we got all we could carry of the food baskets and quilts and tools loaded into our arms and waited by the wagon. When he got back with the lantern we started for the house, about a field's length from where the wagon was stopped. It was cold and wet but we had to take our shoes off so as to not leave them sucked off in the mud behind us. You couldn't tell what you were stepping into, you couldn't hardly stay standing.

It was my dream about the riverbank and the iron pot. Except that Robbie was holding onto me and Tom was up ahead with the lantern, and Virgil and Doug coming up behind so nobody could get lost. Soon as we got within hearing range, Virgil and Robbie started calling out for Mama and Daddy. Nothing. I don't know how long it took us to get up onto the porch. They all stood around for a minute scraping mud off, then Virgil put his hand on the doorknob. Virgil looked over to me before he went in.

"The house is dry, Linney," he said. "The house is dry. Nobody has drowned inside the house." I nodded and kept holding onto Robbie.

"Alright?" Virgil asked. I nodded again and he went inside. We could hear him walking through, opening doors and saying "Carl? Rose? Betts?" He come back to the door and held it open.

"Not a soul in sight," he said. "Let's come on in and get settled and see what we can think to do."

"That can't be right," I told him. It couldn't be I'd got through last night and the trip here and the walk from the wagon to the house and still didn't know what had gone on. Still couldn't say all that needed said. "We have to find them."

"We will," Virgil said. He looked about as serious as a body could look. "But we can't do anything till morning. We're going to get us a fire going and get warm and dry and get some food in us. Come morning we'll be able see a lot better what to do."

We did like Virgil said. I looked around the front room and kitchen while they seen about the fire and the food. It looked so strange and so familiar all at the same time. The furniture in the front room was moved around, and one of the benches from the kitchen table was moved in there. There was lots of food in the kitchen, more than we usually kept, and it was all cleaned up.

"Does it feel wrong to you?" I asked Robbie, and he said it did.

Nobody wanted to sleep in any of the beds, me either. We made pallets out of the quilts and blankets Pearl and Aunt Hesty had piled into the wagon, and we all slept together on the floor in the front room.

I dreamed again I was in the kitchen with the empty drawers in the house everybody knew was haunted. This time in the dream, it was coming on to night. I heard a door slam and I was so scared and thinking I should have known better than to move into the house. I'd been tricked by what a fine house it was—so many rooms, a nice big porch and windows everywhere—but it was somebody else's house and now, living or dead, they was back. Such a good house was not for me, I was just a squatter. I run quick through the house but there was no back door. The rooms was all empty, there was no place to hide from whatever it was that slammed the door. I hunkered down in a corner and listened for footsteps coming toward me, but none come.

Then I knew, the way you know things sometimes in dreams, that the slamming door was not the sound of someone or something coming in, but the sound of something going out. There was another little part then, in the dream, but one of the boys moved, or the wood shifted in the fire and woke me and I couldn't hold onto it. Besides that, I didn't remember a thing till morning.

I woke up tired, but with my heart beating a mile a minute. Virgil had just dropped an armful of wood in the front of the fire and was stirring around in the coals, fixing to warm up the house. He seen me sitting up. "Robbie's bringing in stove wood for the kitchen," he said, "you think you can get us some coffee going?"

I half thought Mama would be in the kitchen when I got in there. I got the coffee started and set some cups on the table. Then some plates and one of the baskets of wedding food. The biscuits was hard on the outside, but when I broke one open it was alright on the inside. I got the butter out of the cupboard to make it better. I didn't like being alone in that kitchen. I called through the house to see if Robbie was inside, but it was Virgil that come into the kitchen. He poured a cup of coffee and sat down at the table with me.

"Could you tell anything when you was outside?" I asked him.

"There's three horses, right?" Virgil asked. I nodded. "Well, Robbie took two with the wagon to come up for the wedding, and the other one's not in the barn."

"What does that mean?"

"Probably somebody rode off on him," Virgil said. "Or Linney, if it was bad trouble, they might have cut him loose to save himself. It don't look like that though, honey. There's some inches of standing water out by the river, but no signs it flooded all the way."

I just stared at him. I didn't know what to say, I didn't know anything at all.

"Listen," Virgil said. "We'll eat and we'll finish having a look around the place, me and the boys—they're out there right now looking around. If we still can't figure nothing out, we'll send Tom out to the

Stokes's place. Robbie says that's the nearest place and if any of them had to ride out for help, that's where they would have gone. At least the Stokes's ought to be able to tell us something about how it was, with the river and all."

"You're alright," he said, when I didn't answer. "We got you and you're alright, Linney."

"Yes," I said, but I'd had about as much not-knowing as I could take. "Send Tom now, Virgil."

He set his cup of coffee down on the table. "He's gone back out to the barn to see what needs done out there, I'll go tell him right now."

I took the coffee pot off the stove and sat back down at the table. I looked around at the kitchen and wisht it wasn't so clean, wisht there was something for me to do, anything that would feel like setting things straight. Some dirty pots I could bang around.

"Linney," Virgil was back too soon, standing in the kitchen doorway with his hat in his hand. "Honey, you better come out here."

It had happened the day before the wedding. Daddy got up and rode into Williamson first thing to see if he could hear anything about what was going on up and down the river, what with the rain and all. He must have heard the same thing the preacher told us, about the river full and rushing and felling trees along the bank. All the rest of that day he sat out on the porch watching, and when it started getting dark and he couldn't see, he went down there with a lantern. He was afraid a tree would go down and dam it up down there and overrun the tobacco field.

He knew that was not a good place for the tobacco, but it was the ground him and Robbie could clear fastest for it.

He stayed out there, and Mama didn't like it, but she didn't get scared when it got to be bedtime and he didn't come in. She knew it to be like him, to stand out there like he could do something about a river bringing down a tree. Like he could stave it off.

She looked out from the porch and seen the lantern still lit out there before she went to bed. Come morning, he was not in the bed. When she looked out that way from the porch, she seen the big willow was down but she couldn't see him. She hollered to Betts and run down there to the river in her bare feet and nightgown. The lantern was sitting on the ground and no sign of him anywhere. She waded in, screaming for Daddy, trying to hold on to the willow, first along the upstream side as far as she could, then the downstream side, but she couldn't see nor feel any sign of him. She slipped and went a few yards downstream, then made it to the bank, who knows how. She screamed Betts down off the porch and to the barn and the two of them rode off on the one horse to the Stokes place, as fast as the horse could go.

What Virgil had called me out to the porch to see was Mr. Stokes coming up the road with Mama and Betts in his wagon. When I seen just the two of them coming back, I still didn't know just what had happened, but I knew it was Daddy it'd happened to. I took ahold of the porchrail.

"Good thinking," I was hearing from someplace inside my head, "Keep a cool head, Linney." And Daddy sitting at the kitchen table across from me that morning he told us his plan about sending me away, saying, easy like it was nothing, "It won't be forever, Linney."

Robbie and Doug come and stood on either side of me. Mama started talking soon as they got down off the wagon, it seemed like she couldn't stop telling it. Betts started telling some things too, about that morning—how Mama sounded, screaming, and how it scared her. When Betts started in on that, Mama just give out.

"Rose, Rose," Virgil said, and that was all he had in him to say. He'd moved over to stand behind me, keeping a hand on each of my shoulders.

Tom and Robbie got Mama onto the porch swing, Betts too, and Doug went in and brought out coffee and water.

"They need to eat," Mr. Stokes said to Virgil, and the boys went in and brought out plates filled with what all I had set out on the table. Mama was doubled over in the swing like her stomach was hurting, rocking back and forth, crying without making any noise. Betts was staring at me.

"Bring them quilts out of the livingroom," Virgil told the boys and they did that too. Mr. Stokes went ahead and told the rest of it.

He'd brought his boys and a couple of horses and good rope and between them, they pulled the willow out of the river. Daddy come out with it. "Either he fell in, not being able to see the bank clear in the dark," Mr. Stokes said, "or else he waded in there and tried to push the tree clear enough to let the water by."

I looked at Mama. I knew what he did.

"Anyway," Mr. Stokes went on, "we carried him up here and cleaned him up best we could and laid him out on the kitchen table. Then we had to go back home. Rose already knew," he said. "But some things you don't know you know all the way till you've got to." He took his hat off and wiped his face. "Folks come and we had a kind of a praying, not a preaching for the preacher had gone on. We had to bury him that same day." He looked at Virgil and wiped his face again. "We had to."

Sometimes nothing is happening and that's all there is to it. And sometimes nothing is happening and it takes up all the air in the house. The first few days, everywhere I looked, Daddy was not blowing on his cup of coffee, nor sitting and figuring, nor standing in the doorway telling what all he'd done that day.

I was still sleeping out in the front room with Virgil and the boys, and Mama and Betts was sleeping together in Mama and Daddy's room. Virgil and the boys was going out every day and working on cleaning up the barn. Water had got in there too, six inches or so, just enough to make a good mess and ruin some of the low boards on the outside walls and the stalls. There was a big cleanup to be done in the tobacco field too, raking up what was left of the plants that drowned out there. When I wanted to get out of the house, I'd go see if there was any of it I could help with, or else just find a way to sit out where they was working.

Betts was sleeping a lot in the day, sometimes back in our old bedroom, sometimes in one of the chairs in the front room. Just as well. I'm not saying she wasn't hurt—how would I know what was going on inside her? But when she was up and wandering around and one of the boys come into sight, she'd start into sighing so pitiful that you couldn't take it serious. The boys would turn and go the other way if they seen her coming.

Mama, on the other hand, couldn't stop moving around the house. She got up and made breakfast every morning, stepping over all of us in the front room to get into the kitchen before daylight. She wouldn't stop the whole day long then, scrubbing everything in the house and talking to herself about things she picked up, what she needed and what she didn't. One morning I walked into the front room and she was holding a little clock from the mantel in her hand, up in front of her face, staring at it. She turned to look at me, turned from her feet without shifting anything else about her body or how she was holding that clock.

"I forgot," she said, "you're supposed to stop the clocks."

"You can do that if you want to, Mama," I said, and I went over to stand beside her, took the clock from her and was looking at the back of it to figure out how to do it.

She pulled it away, put it back behind her back. "No," she said. "It's mine now. I want my time, Linney—" She brought the clock back around and held it in both hands in front of her where we both could see it. She caught the end of her sleeve between her fingers and her palm and wiped dust off the face. More to the clock than to me, she said, "I want my time."

Then she looked up like she was surprised I was there and went on with her cleaning and putting things in order. That went on for some days. At night, after her and Betts went to bed, Virgil would ask me how Mama was doing and I would tell him, good enough.

"How about you, honey?" he asked.

"Alright," I said. "No. I don't know. I couldn't explain it if I tried."

"You don't have to explain nothing, Linney," Virgil said, and he didn't look at my face when he said it. It was as kind a thing as anyone could have done for me.

In those first days, what I what I mostly felt for Daddy was sorry. I've not held very many babies, just sometimes at church, but there is something about it that is different from anything else. When you're holding a baby, it's like you've got a whole life in your hands. A life entire, that you can hold and lift up to your shoulder and feel how small and how big it is all at the same time. I never knew somebody that died before, but there was something about it that felt the same as holding those babies. Daddy's life was entire now because it was over, you could see all its edges, you could hold it and look at it.

You could see where he thought and did so big, and you could see where he stayed small and was held by things that was bigger than him. Like his own Daddy telling him daylight was wasting. Then him sending me off, telling me, "Now this makes sense. People do it all the time."

I wisht he'd sat down and fished with Robbie that morning. Maybe if he would have just sat beside the river every once in a while, he'd not have had to die in it the way he did.

Sometime in that first week, two of Daddy's brothers come down to see us. We didn't hardly know them, for they had moved even farther north than Chandlers and more off to the west after their daddy died and left everything to Daddy. I couldn't figure how they got word, but there they was, standing at the front door with their hats in their hands and looking like two other versions of Daddy. Short and muscled, them same blue eyes and squared jaws. It did my eyes good to see them. John and Burt was their names.

They shuffled and looked around a lot, it was hard for any of us to know what to say. We brought them cups of coffee and some cake one of the neighbor women had brought. It was the middle of the morning. Finally, Uncle John, he was the eldest, he leaned forward in his chair.

"Rose," he said to Mama, "we've come to talk about some things."

She rocked back in her rocker and held it from rocking back forward again with her foot. She looked all around the room, how it was all cleaned and set into place. The room got so quiet you could hear the clock ticking. Then she let the rocker rock forward and stood up.

"Come on into the kitchen, then," she said. "We can think better in there."

They didn't ask me to come with them, but I went in anyway and took my place at the table. Betts come in, too. "Go get Virgil from the barn," I told her, and she went and brought him back while Mama was getting more coffee on and the rest of us was sitting and waiting to start. The men all shook hands. Uncle John and Uncle Burt sat on one side of the table, me and Mama and Virgil and Betts sat across from them.

Uncle John leaned forward and tapped the tips of his fingers together, just like Daddy did. I wasn't sure I could sit still for it, whatever it was that was coming. He looked at Mama and me and Betts.

"It's a terrible thing," he said, "has happened to you."

Mama made a noise like crying, if crying went inside you like a twisty knife instead of coming out like it's supposed to.

"Me and Burt, here," he said, "we're feeling it too, it don't matter what come before." Uncle Burt pressed the heels of his hands against his eyes, then wiped down his face and kept his eyes down on the table.

I tried to think if I ever saw Daddy cry. Maybe once. I'd walked into his and Mama's room not knowing he was in there, right after he'd got back from Pikeville that one year we had such a puny crop.

"Now, I got three boys," Uncle John went on.

I felt like the floor was falling away. I grabbed onto the crook of Virgil's arm, and he covered my hand with his.

"There's still the farm to be worked, and there's a lot happening down here, what with the railroad and the mines and all," Uncle John said. "What we're thinking Rose, if you're willing, is we'd like to come back down here, and figure some ways for us all to be in on it together."

Mama was staring at them, but it was not a blank stare, I could see she was hearing what they was saying. I could see she was considering.

"Now, Novi, that's my wife," Uncle Burt says, "she's been hankering for a change for a while now. She don't like it so much out there back of beyond where we are, she likes people around. Now we've not had no more time to think about things than the trip down here. But if me and John sold our places, we'd have some cash money for starting up something in town. Maybe a boarding house, maybe between you and Burt's Alice and Novi, and all our girls together, you could get that going. And we'd be working the farm, all us men, and that'd be food for us and the boarding house plus whatever we could sell."

It was almost exactly what Daddy wanted, except for the all-of-us-together part. We all sat there a minute, looking down at our coffee and back and forth at each other in quick little looks.

"You think about it," Uncle John said to Mama. "We're going to stay over in Williamson for a few days and see what it's like. If we was to come back on Friday, you think you'd be ready to talk about it? I'm not asking you to have an answer by then, now," he said, "just to talk, and only if you're ready."

Mama nodded.

"Well, then, we'll go on and let you be to talk and think about it," Uncle John said. He got up from the table and Uncle Burt did too. Uncle Burt winked at me, not a funny wink, slow and serious enough to be a hug. "Unless you got anything you want to say right now," Uncle John turned back around at the kitchen doorway to ask Mama.

"It's good to see you," she said, and that was all. They went on and me and Mama and Virgil and Betts went back to the kitchen to sit. Mama wasn't talking, but she was thinking.

"Be pretty easy to add on to this house, a couple rooms maybe, till you got another one built, if you needed to," Virgil said. "Me and the boys could come do it for you, even before winter sets all the way in." He was looking all around the room, but he stopped that and fixed on Mama. "Or else, Rose, I expect you know you and Betts can come stay with us, long as you need."

"And Linney," Mama said, but she was still thinking her way down the other path. "Me and Betts and Linney, you mean."

Virgil's face twitched, but Mama wasn't looking at him. "Yes," he said. "I'm going back out to the barn and see how they're doing." He looked at me. "You need anything, you let me know."

Mama slowed down in her cleaning and moving things around after that. But she kept moving around the house, touching things, standing back in the corner of a room and looking out on all the things in it. Taking stock, I think. One morning, I seen her standing in the front room, feeling the wall by the front door, her palms flat against it like a person feeling for a way out in the dark. It was just me and her in the house.

"Mama," I asked her, "what are you doing?"

"Feeling the walls," she said. "They're solid, I think." She turned around, her face looked all shadowed even though it was just ordinary morning light in the room.

"It wasn't none of this my fault."

"I know, Mama," I said, for I did know nobody could've stopped Daddy from going into the river. I stood back from her so she could keep on. I wanted to hear whatever she wanted to say.

"It turns out," she said, "that means it wasn't none of it my doing either."

"I don't know what you mean."

"It's almost like a trick. You go along thinking to yourself, 'I didn't do it, I didn't do it' till you come up on something you can't get around and it smacks you right in the face—you didn't do wrong things, but you never did the right things neither."

She turned back around and pressed her palms flat against the wall again. "And there's all these walls."

She wasn't talking about the wall that had growed up between us, but that's what I was feeling. And I didn't know if I wanted to knock it down or build it up.

I had not felt for my penny the whole time I'd been here and all of a sudden I was afraid it might be gone, but it was there where I'd pinned it. My penny was the doll in my pocket. I held onto it till I heard that voice, then I walked up behind Mama slow, put my hands on her waist, and moved her over, just two steps to the left.

"And doors," I said.

I let go of her waist and she walked through.

"And doors," she said.

Then she looked back at me like I could tell her what just happened.

Something, but not enough, I knew that much. Not until she could see the place she'd given me—or not given me—in the whole story. She was still looking to me to figure out something that was her mess, hers and Daddy's.

I was in Aunt Hesty's story about Lissa, when she tells the granny woman "I'm not doing that. I'll do my own work."

That was a long morning for us. We stayed out on the back porch, Mama talked and I listened. Mostly it was about her mama and daddy, and what all she thought about when she was a girl. I already had a pretty good idea of what that was all about from Aunt Hesty, so as I was listening, I was trying to hold that story together with what was happening right then.

"Daddy wanted milk with his breakfast," she was saying, "so I was standing in the doorway holding one end of a rope Mama had tied around her waist so she could walk out to the barn in a snowstorm and get it for him. I must have been about Betts's age, but I knew it didn't make any sense. I was starting to get real mad about things when your daddy come along and he wanted to do things, he wanted to do everything.

I did too. But come to find out, he was fixing to do it all hisself. And he did. In the beginning, though, I thought it would be us, doing together."

She stopped to take a drink out of her coffee cup.

"Mama," I asked, "what do you want to do now?"

She looked down into her cup. "I'm so tired," she said, and she let her head drop back against the back of the chair. She raised it back up and looked out across the cornfield, then at me, then back out at the field. The sky was so changeable that morning, the field was flashing back and forth between golden and done-for. "Almost anything," she answered the morning around us, more than me. "Almost anything, long as it's mine."

The next morning when we was setting out breakfast, Mama asked me "How many people you think would actually fit around this table?" She found something in the wedding food basket, some kind of little cakes, and she said, "Now, that looks like something people would like," and she asked Virgil if he knew who made them. I figured she was getting pictures in her head of how it could be, the uncles' plan. But there was other kinds of moments, too, when you'd walk into a room and find her standing there staring into nothing.

"What are you doing, Mama?" I asked when I found her that way one morning in the kitchen.

"I don't know," she said. "Linney, I don't know what to do, not even where to put my feet. Last night I dreamed I couldn't find my hands."

My heart was like the cornfield, that morning me and mama sat out on the porch and she told her stories—flashing back and forth between gold and dark. Golden for when I could almost feel what it would be like to go home to stay. Dark like a covered bridge all the times I was watching for a chance to get Mama alone and able to listen, to tell her that I wasn't staying here. I was going to feel like a snared rabbit till I got that over with. It had to happen before the uncles come back and she give them her answer.

I went looking for Robbie. He was out in the barn working with the rest of them, but he set down his saw when he seen me and nudged Tom to look over at me there in the doorway. Tom nodded and give me a smile, and Robbie come on over to me, shaking sawdust out of his clothes as he come.

"How's it coming?" I asked him. I pointed out between the fields, where we could walk and nobody much see us.

"Good," he said. "The barn will be all back good by the end of the day, and the field by the river's all cleaned up. We raked a big pile out at the edge of the woods, we'll probably burn that before we go so it's left all nice and clean. Nothing much else to do."

"Good," I said.

"You talk to your mama yet?"

"Every time I get her alone, she's all in pieces," I said. "I can't talk to her when she's like that." We kept walking, it was more like pacing. Neither of us said anything for a long while.

"What do you think you'll do?" he said when we got to the edge of the woods and turned left to walk in the little track in between the woods and the field.

They say that when you're drowning, your whole life flashes before your eyes. I was seeing so many pictures in my head, just whipping by—Daddy and Mama and Betts, Robbie and me out behind the house, everything that happened to me since. And then I remembered that lost bit of dream from the first night I'd been back in the house. The empty drawer, haunted house dream where the door had slammed, and I'd been so scared that something was coming to get me. I'd stood up from the corner I was sitting in, in the dream, and gone to the door to look out.

It was Daddy out in the yard, walking toward the river. In the dream, Daddy had turned around when he heard the screen door slap closed behind me. I hadn't seen at first what he was carrying, but he raised a fishing pole up in the air, give it a little shake to wave at me, and smiled. "Good thinking!" he called to me across the yard then turned back around and went on his way.

"I don't know," I said. "I don't know how, but I think I've got to do it right now."

"Linney," he said. "Go."

I turned and started walking fast back toward the house, but turned around after a few steps without hardly knowing what I was doing.

"Robbie. What do you think you'll do?"

"I'll wait here."

"I mean, you know, after."

"Be home," he said. "For a good long while. That's all I know."

I found Mama in mine and Betts' old room. I'd not even seen the door to that room open since I got back, as I'd been sleeping out with the boys and Betts had been sleeping with Mama in her room. She was sitting on my bed, that lost look on her. I knelt down on the floor in front of her. The room felt cold to me, like there was nothing living in it, like that snakeskin Aunt Hesty pointed out to me on our way back from the place.

"We can't stay in here, Mama," I said to her, though that was not at all how I thought we'd start.

"I'm not ready," she said.

"There's no such thing," I told her. I put my hand in my pocket, no idea in my head of what to say next. I pulled the wrapped-up penny out of my pocket, like I might be able to hear it better if I could see it.

"What is that?" Mama asked. I put it in her hand and wrapped her fingers around it and held them tight. It was the iron pot, the borrowed fire. Maybe I'd brought it home after all. Maybe that was what I had to do to get myself this last bit of the way to what I really wanted.

"The boys are all out in the barn," I said. "Let's go sit in the kitchen a bit, Mama. I need to tell you some things." We got us some coffee and a couple sweet things still left from the food baskets. I told her almost everything.

"You sound so different, Linney," she said.

"I am, Mama, and I'm not. There's more of me, but I still am who I am."

She looked at me, and then looked away. There was that little square of light coming through on the kitchen floor, she put her foot out on it like she was trying to see it better.

I remembered what Danny said, about how the time to leave comes and you just know there's really nothing else you can do. I remembered when they told us they were sending me away, how careless Daddy'd been, talking about who was removed, not even thinking what it meant. Mama did know, and she let it happen anyway.

She still wasn't looking me in the eye.

"Mama, look at me," I said. I was still her daughter. But I would not be the daughter of her wrongs. "I cannot stay here. You know why."

She sat staring into her cup of coffee, I don't know how long. I didn't speak, I waited. The next words between us was up to her.

"You don't know what it is to be married, Linney, and you only know the half of how your Daddy was. No stopping him once he got started."

Her whole body drew back from me, her face was awful.

"If it hurt you so bad to leave then, why not come back? How is it not wrong now? I never thought this of you, Linney, that you could be so cruel as to leave me in such a state. You tell me, what's the difference then, between what happened then and what you're doing to me now?"

"The difference"—it felt like my mouth was saying this without me—"is that I'm grown now." I made myself look her in the eye. "And you are the mother. All that's happened, Mama, and you're still the same. You think you see me, but you don't. How can you think you love somebody when you can't even see who they are?"

"Well," she said. She sat staring at me for a minute or so, then stood up and walked back through the house to the doorway of mine and Betts's old bedroom. I followed her.

"Leave me be," she said. "Just a little while, Linney."

She rolled over onto her side on my old bed, away from me. Wasn't a thing in the world else I could do for her, so I stood up to leave..

"Can I leave the door open?" I asked her, "so you don't freeze?"

"Leave it cracked," she said, "but don't let nobody come in."

I sat out in the front room, even though that meant I could hear her, and waved everybody away, back out to the porch, or into the kitchen. When it got to be suppertime I walked over to the door, but I didn't look in.

"I'll get supper on," I said. "You come on out if you feel like it. I'll bring you a plate if you don't."

Betts come around while I was in the kitchen. "Where's Mama?" she asked.

"Resting," I said. I looked at her, considering. I handed her a knife and nodded at her to sit and help me with the potatoes.

"Can you even do potatoes?" she asked me. That sneaky, downturned smile of hers, that voice she used, I had not missed that one bit.

But her back was to the doorway and she hadn't seen Virgil come in, the boys not far behind him, so pleased she was with that bit of meanness. Virgil come up behind her and he put one hand on each of her shoulders. Not hard, Virgil didn't need to be hard. People heard what he was telling them because of who he was. There was not a false thing about him.

"How are you, young lady?" he said to her.

She looked up at him out from under her eyelashes, like she always did when she thought she was putting something over on somebody.

"It's so hard." She said it with a little tremble in her voice.

"I couldn't be sorrier for what your family's going through," Virgil said, and I could see he meant it.

She give him a little simpery smile and I seen the boys rolling their eyes.

Virgil patted one of her shoulders twice then took his hands away. "One more thing, young lady. You speak to Linney like that again, it's me you'll answer to."

Tom cleared his throat real loud, so Betts would know they none of them would have it. Then they got what they needed from the kitchen and went on out back to work.

Seemed like Betts didn't quite know how to look at me, so she didn't look at me at all.

She picked up the knife and started on the potatoes. "I just really didn't know if you could do it," she said. It was a lie, but I didn't need to waste any words to call her on it.

Mama did come out for supper. Her face was all splotched and pale, but she was quiet in a new way. It felt to me like the kind of quiet I had that morning after I had gone up to the clearing to cry, before the Chandlers come and got me. If that was what it was, it was a kind of quiet she could start out from.

When the uncles come back, they couldn't hardly keep their eyes off Mama's face, looking for signs of what her answer would be. We all of us got settled around the table the way we was before. She didn't wait to be asked.

"I may not be good for much for a while, but after that I might be good for a lot, I don't know," she said.

"If you can live with that, then yes."

The uncles let out big breaths, then they hugged on each other still sitting there on the bench. You could feel all through the kitchen how gone Daddy was.

"Rose—" Uncle John begun.

"I know," she said. "Don't talk about it now."

So they didn't. They begun to talk about what they was figuring, and what all they'd found out in Williamson. They'd got a good idea of what they might get for their places, enough, Uncle Burt said, to buy a big house outright in Williamson on the West Virginia side, just across the river for a boarding house, and to put it right on the inside with furniture and dishes and linens and such as that. They'd heard people could make good money that way.

"But would me and Mama still live here?" Betts asked.

"You all can work it out," Uncle Burt said, "however you need, but we was imagining with the seven of you ladies and girls, you might take turns staying over and doing in the house and here at home. We don't know, you all will see what works best all the way around."

"Six," Mama said. Now it was Virgil that let out a big breath.

"Uh—" Uncle John said, started out to count us out on his fingers.

Mama didn't look at Virgil nor at me. I waited to see which one of us was going to have to say it out loud.

"I'm going home with Virgil and the boys," I said when the silence at the table got to be too much.

Then Mama went on real fast, to talk about the next thing. I heard them talking about adding on rooms to the house, about another house on the place.

Virgil was joining in to say what all him and the boys could do, and to tell what all he'd been hearing about the railroad and mines and things in town. You could almost see it all on the table in front of us—houses and rooms, trips into town, all kinds of people coming in and out. Uncle John would stay here with Mama while Uncle Burt went back and took care of getting everything and everybody ready to come down. Some weeks, they thought it would take.

After a while, my ears got couldn't take in any more talk about all the new things. I stood up.

"You alright, Linney?" Virgil said.

I nodded. "I just need some air," I said. Mama told me to get a sweater on so I did, it didn't cost me nothing to do what she wanted. The boys was all out on the back porch, waiting to hear what was going on.

"She said yes," I told them, but that was not what they was waiting to hear. "I bet we can start home tomorrow or the next day," I said.

They all nodded, then Robbie whooped like at the wedding, only a lot quieter so they wouldn't hear him inside, and hugged me up off my feet and swung me around, then Tom did and Doug too. We sat out there on the porch talking about home and Danny and Delsie till they called us in for dinner.

Uncle John and Uncle Burt stayed the night. They slept in mine and Betts' old room and that seemed alright. Come morning, there was not much talk. Me and Mama packed up baskets for the road, for Uncle Burt and for us. I was covering up one of the baskets with a cloth when Mama come up beside me and put her hand on mine.

"Linney," she said.

It was still true, what I knew before we come down here and found out about Daddy, about there being two sides to the penny. It was not nothing, this leaving. Mama held me hard, I could feel something in her trying to reach me. I let her hug me, but it was different for me. It was not her I needed. It was no use for me pretending things was any different from what they were.

When she let loose, looked like she maybe felt a bit better. We straightened ourselves out before anybody come in. The penny, still wrapped up in the cloth, fell out of her apron pocket when she lifted her apron tail up to wipe her face.

She held it up between thumb and finger. "What do I do with it, Linney?" she asked me. "What's it mean?"

"It's yours," I told her. "That's what it means."

HOME

OCTOBER 1910

IT WAS ALMOST DARK when we got home. We'd only stopped once on the way, to eat and give the horses a rest. We seen another wagon outside the barn when we got close enough to see. Virgil said it was probably Mr. Marcus's wagon and that made sense since we knew he'd been coming around and checking on things. They wouldn't know even what day to expect us, so as soon as we got within hearing the boys started hollering out to the house for Pearl and Aunt Hesty and Walt. They all come out to the porch and into the yard toward us and I could see Pearl and Aunt Hesty waving their heads back and forth, to see through the crowd of boys that I was there. I was.

Brother come running up and barking and carrying on so, we couldn't hardly get him off me. I didn't want to get him off me. I said to Pearl, "He can come in, can't he?" and she said he sure could. Said he'd been pacing and crying for days.

And Danny and Delsie was there too, we never even thought of that, but they'd started coming down with Mr. Marcus of an evening. Danny was helping Mr. Marcus and Walt, and Delsie was keeping Pearl and Aunt Hesty company while they waited them days for us to get back. Mr. Marcus had gone down to

Paintsville to see if there was any word about us and our place, so they already knew about Daddy.

"We didn't know," Pearl said, "if you'd come straight back or if you'd need a little time."

"I knowed," Aunt Hesty said.

It was a lot of talk then, and it was sweet to my ears. Pearl and Aunt Hesty kept putting their hands on me every time they was close enough. We had supper all together at the table, with chairs brought in from the porch to make enough places. Aunt Hesty started in on Danny about maybe needing more places soon, but Pearl pinched her arm where everybody could see. It wasn't making him mad anymore anyway. When we got back into the front room, we was all a little more quiet. Aunt Hesty looked at me and arched that eyebrow and nodded over toward the mantel.

"Give me just a minute," I said. I pushed myself out of my chair and went back into my room.

I felt my whole self gather when I walked through that doorway. I sat on my bed and with both hands I smoothed the covers. I laid back flat on my back and looked at the ceiling, then all the walls and sat up and looked at everything there was in that room. I swung my legs over the edge of the bed and sat there a minute, getting ready for what I was about to do. I got down on the floor, reached one arm blind under the bed and pulled out my box that Daddy made me. I sat back up on the bed, smoothing across the top of the lid, first with my topside hand, then with my underneath hand. I traced the letters of my name with my finger, as he'd carved it on the lid, Caroline. I opened it up and took everything out. I left it empty and ready as those drawers in my dream.

I had seen Aunt Hesty check to see to that the ink pen was on the mantel before we all sat down to supper and I snuck it into my pocket, pretending I needed to go in and get warm by the fire. I took it out now. I sat back on the bed with my legs sticking out in front of me and the inside of the lid laying flat across my lap.

I would write my own name inside the box Daddy made, the box for holding my innermost things, whatever the next things would be. Not the name him and Mama give me, Caroline, but Linney-who I was, who I turned out to be.

Before I let Aunt Hesty write it into the family Bible, I had to write it for myself. I had to sign my own name to it.

I wrote it inside, under the lid. Then I traced over it four or five more times, till it wasn't just the ink saying my name, but the grooves that the writing made. I closed the box, then opened the lid just a crack and slid my underneath hand under the lid to make sure I could feel my name with that hand too. Then I closed the box and put it back under my bed. I stood up and straightened my clothes and combed my hair with my fingers. I picked up the pen and went back out to the front room.

Nobody was in the front room, they was all in the kitchen. Aunt Hesty had spread the family tree out on the center of the table. There was a lamp lit at each end of the table and everybody was standing around looking at all the names and waiting for me. Virgil and Pearl was beside Aunt Hesty, and Robbie was on her other side. When I come in, everybody turned and looked at me, and Robbie made room for me to stand there by him.

"I seen you took my pen," Aunt Hesty said. "Let's have it."

I give it to her. She started with Virgil and Pearl and read across all the names like she'd done before. When she come to my space, she looked up at me, sideways how she does. Her eyes was soft and glowy from the lamps, like they'd been in the cave.

"Caroline Marie Stepp, is it? she asked me.

"No," I said, but she was not taken aback like she was before when I'd told her to wait.

"Linney, Linney Stepp," I said. "I come as myself."

"Yes, you do," Aunt Hesty said, and Pearl said "Amen to that."

I watched her hand as she wrote, and I watched the letters as they come onto the page. I knew who I was, and so did they. I was trying to think what I could say, when Brother come running and sliding in and barking up a storm.

"He thinks he's missing the party," Robbie said, and he knelt down to pet him and help him quiet down, but he couldn't quiet down. Robbie looked up grinning. "Brother's right," he said. "It is a party. You got any cake, Mama?"

"I could use some cake," Aunt Hesty said.

"I'm sure I got something," Pearl said. "You need some cake, Linney?"

It fell quiet then, one of them strange quiets where everybody seems to stop talking all at once. Even Brother quieted down and looked at me, his head tilted over to one side, how dogs do when they're waiting for an answer.

Virgil was standing with his arm around Pearl and everybody was looking at me again. Virgil cleared his throat a time or two.

"You need any cake, Linney, " he said, "you let us know."

They all nodded, so serious. Then Danny pushed Virgil a little bit sideways and they all started grinning.

I was grinning too. Brother was barking again and I was laughing.

"Oh, I do," I promised. "I will."

Acknowledgments

Ongoing thanks and love to the AROHO community and Darlene Chandler Bassett. The first draft of this book was written with the financial support of the Gift of Freedom and the ontinuing friendship of the A Room of Her Own Foundation. Eleanor Wilner was a reader for me during that time and is a dear and brilliant companion always.

My renshi sisters, George Ella Lyon, Melva Sue Priddy, and Ruth Thompson are indispensable presences in my life, as is my brother Doug Van Gundy.

Ruth Thompson and Don Mitchell at Saddle Road Press have helped me bring Linney into the world, and with Ruth's invaluable editing and suggestions, she has been able to say all that she needed to say.

About Diane Gilliam

Diane Gilliam has published four poetry collections: *Dreadful Wind & Rain, Kettle Bottom, One of Everything,* and *Recipe for Blackberry Cake,* a chapbook. Her work has earned a Pushcart Prize, the Ohioana Library Association Book of the Year in Poetry, the 2008 Chaffin Award for Appalachian Writing, and the Gift of Freedom for the A Room of Her Own Foundation.

She lives and writes in Akron, Ohio, and teaches in regional writing workshops, and in the low-residency MFA program at West Virginia Wesleyan College. This is her first novel.

Printed in the USA
CPSIA information can be obtained
at www.ICGtesting.com
LVHW041041171023
761337LV00002B/65

9 781736 525883